THE HOUSE THAT KILLS

LA MAISON QUI TUE

Paul Halter books from Locked Room International
The Lord of Misrule (2010)
The Fourth Door (2011)
The Seven Wonders of Crime (2011)
The Demon of Dartmoor (2012)
The Seventh Hypothesis (2012)
The Tiger's Head (2013)
The Crimson Fog (2013)
The Night of the Wolf (2013)*
The Invisible Circle (2014)
The Picture from the Past (2014)

*Original short story collection published by Wildside Press (2006)

Other impossible crime novels from Locked Room International:
The Riddle of Monte Verita (Jean-Paul Torok) 2012
The Killing Needle (Henry Cauvin) 2014
The Derek Smith Omnibus (Derek Smith) 2014

Visit our website at www.mylri.com or
www.lockedroominternational.com

THE HOUSE THAT KILLS

Noel Vindry

Translated by John Pugmire

The House That Kills

This book is a work of fiction. The characters, incidents, and dialogue are drawn from the author's imagination and are not to be construed as real. Any resemblance to actual events or persons, living or dead, is entirely coincidental.

First published in French in 1932 by
Les Chefs-d'œuvre du Roman d'Aventures as *La Maison qui tue*
© *Editions GALLIMARD, Paris, 1932*
THE HOUSE THAT KILLS
English translation copyright © by John Pugmire 2015

Cover design by Joseph Gérard

All rights reserved. No part of this book may be used or reproduced in any manner whatsoever without written permission except in the case of brief quotations embodied in critical articles and reviews.

For information, contact: pugmire1@yahoo.com

FIRST AMERICAN EDITION
Library of Congress Cataloging-in-Publication Data
Vindry, Noel
[*La Maison qui tue*. English]
The House That Kills / Noel Vindry
Translated from the French by John Pugmire

FOREWORD

Noel Vindry (1896-1954), wrote twelve locked room novels between 1932 and 1937, of a quality and quantity to rival his contemporary, John Dickson Carr (1905-1977), the American writer generally acknowledged to be the master of the sub-genre. Yet today Vindry remains largely forgotten by the French-speaking world and almost completely unknown in the English-speaking.

I first learned about Noel Vindry from Roland Lacourbe, the noted French locked room expert and anthologist, who calls him "the French John Dickson Carr." Much of what follows is taken from *Enigmatika No. 39: Noel Vindry*, a private publication edited by Jacques Baudou, Roland Lacourbe and Michel Lebrun, with a contribution from the author's son, Georges Vindry.

Noel Vindry came from an old Lyon family from whom he inherited his passion for culture and gourmet cuisine. Shortly after acquiring a bachelor's degree he enlisted in the army, where he fought with distinction, earning a *Croix de Guerre*, but was invalided out in 1915 with severe lung damage.

During his long convalescence he studied and mastered law sufficiently to become a deputy *juge d'instruction* (examining magistrate)—a position unique to countries practising the Napoleonic Code, under which a single jurist is given total authority over a case, from investigating crime scenes to questioning witnesses; from ordering the arrest of suspects to preparing the prosecution's case, if any (see Appendix 1.)

He was appointed to serve in Aix-en-Provence in the south of France which, at the time, boasted the second largest Appeals Court outside of Paris, and which he chose because of its climate. Known as the "city of a thousand fountains," it holds a music festival every year to rival those of Bayreuth, Glyndebourne and Salzburg. In Vindry's time, it was known as *La Belle Dormante (Sleeping Beauty)* because "at night you can hear the grass growing in the streets," according to Georges Vindry.

His first novel, *La Maison Qui Tue (The House That Kills),* appeared in 1932, the same year as Carr's fourth, *The Waxworks Murder*. Both books featured detectives who were *juges d'instruction:* Vindry's Monsieur Allou and Carr's Henri Bencolin. Vindry's narrator, Lugrin, is the same age as his creator when he entered chambers, but there are few other autobiographical touches.

Vindry's book and the others that swiftly followed attracted considerable interest and, by the mid-1930s, he was one of the three most successful mystery writers in the French-speaking world, along with the two Belgian authors Georges Simenon and Stanislas-André Steeman. He is the only one of the three never to have had his books translated into English (until now) or brought to the screen.

In France, Vindry was hailed as the undisputed master of the "puzzle novel *(roman problème),*" a term he himself coined. In an essay on the detective novel *(Le Roman Policier)* written in 1933 (See Appendix 2), he distinguished between the adventure novel (1); the police novel; and the puzzle novel. The first deals with the acts of the criminal; the second with the arrest of the criminal; and the third with the discovery of the criminal.

He held that the puzzle novel should be constructed like a mathematical problem: at a certain point, which is emphasised, all the clues have been provided fairly, and the rigorous solution will become evident to the astute reader. Allou himself is a deliberately dry figure about whom we learn very little. The plot and the puzzle are everything. Descriptive passages, even of entire countrysides, are kept to two or three sentences; there is not a word about characters' feelings (the omnipresent dialogue allows people to define themselves.)

Already by 1934 there were rumblings from French critics that the puzzle novel, as so consummately practiced by Noel Vindry, failed to give full rein to character development.

(1) That is, detective and criminal adventure in the manner of Edgar Wallace (1875-1932), the prolific British author of The Four Just Men and 174 other books.

In vain had Vindry pointed out in his essay the previous year that: "The detective novel, as opposed to the psychological one, does not see the interior but only the exterior. 'States of mind' are prohibited, because the culprit must remain hidden." Nevertheless, the prominent critic Robert Brasillach asserted in *Marianne* (April, 1934) that the reign of the puzzle novel was already over and there were no more tricks left with which to bamboozle the jaded reader! (For the record, this was before Carr's *The Hollow Man* in 1935; Carter Dickson's *The Judas Window* and Clayton Rawson's *Death from a Top Hat* in 1938; and Pierre Boileau's *Six Crimes Sans Assassin*, with its six impossible murders, in 1939.) It was time to embrace crime novels rich with characterisation and atmosphere—such as those written by a certain M. Georges Simenon, for example.

Simenon, as is well-known, disdained the puzzle novel (despite having written several good puzzle short stories in his early career as Georges Sim) because he saw it as too rigid and too much under the influence of Anglo-Saxon writers. In his novels, the plot and the puzzle—if there is one—are a distant second to atmosphere and the psychology of the characters: the complete antithesis of Vindry's works. And, to further distance himself from the classical detective fiction of the period, it is the humble policeman and not the gifted amateur or the high functionary who solves the case. Thus were the seeds of the police procedural planted at the very peak of the Golden Age.

From 1932 to 1937 both Simenon and Vindry wrote at the same frantic rate as John Dickson Carr/Carter Dickson. After that, Vindry wrote only one more puzzle novel before World War II. Even though he announced on a Radio Française broadcast in 1941 that he was abandoning detective fiction because it didn't amuse him any more (see Appendix 2), he nevertheless wrote three more shortly before he died in 1954; none of them featured M. Allou and, after such a long break from his earlier success, his books failed to sell well.

By this time, however, his views had mellowed and he had become more accommodating towards the detective novel, which he defined, in a 1953 letter to the editor of *Mystère-Magazine* (see Appendix 2), as "a mystery drama dominated by logic," and consisting of three elements:

1. A drama, the part with the action

2. A mystery, the poetic part
3. The logic, the intelligent part
"They are terribly difficult to keep in equilibrium. If drama dominates, we fall into melodrama or worse, as everyone knows; if mystery dominates, we finish up with a fairy tale, something altogether different which doesn't obey the same laws of credibility; if logic dominates, the work degenerates into a game, a chess problem or a crossword and it's no longer a novel."

A great example of equilibrium? Gaston Leroux's *Le Mystère de la Chambre Jaune (The Mystery of the Yellow Room)* published in 1908. This, of course, was also declared by Carr to be the greatest locked room mystery of all.

Meanwhile, Simenon powered on and was next rivalled by Boileau-Narcejac. Pierre Boileau and Thomas Narcejac, individually successful as puzzle novel writers, teamed up following an award dinner for Narcejac to which Boileau, as a previous winner, had been invited. Their novels, while maintaining the brilliant puzzle plots dreamt up by Boileau, relaxed the rigid puzzle novel formula espoused by Vindry and incorporated Narcejac's descriptive and character work.

Although he may have been a shooting star, Noel Vindry was much admired by his peers. Steeman, in a letter to Albert Pigasse, the founder of *Le Masque*, in 1953, suggested that, even though Vindry's latest work was his weakest, he deserved a prize which everyone—readers and critics alike—would realise was for the ensemble of his work. Narcejac, writing in *Combat* after Vindry's death in 1954, asserted that nobody, not even "those specialists E. Queen and D. Carr" *(sic),* was the equal of the master, Noel Vindry. Even though the puzzle-novel was well and truly dead, if he had to designate its poet, he would not hesitate: it would be Vindry. And, in their 1964 memoir on *Le Roman Policier* (The Detective Novel), Boileau and Narcejac spoke of his "unequalled virtuosity" and "stupefying puzzles."

If Golden Age Detection needed a patron saint, then Noel Vindry would surely be a candidate.

John Pugmire

ADDENDUM : NOEL VINDRY NOVELS

Les Chefs-d'Oeuvre du Roman d'Aventures* (Gallimard)

La Maison qui tue (The House That Kills) 1932
Le Loup du Grand-Aboy (The Wolf of Grand-Aboy) 1932
La Fuite des morts (Disappearing Bodies) 1933

Hors série (Gallimard)

Le Piège aux diamants (The Diamond Trap) 1933
Le Fantôme de midi (The Ghost of Noon) 1934

Série "M. Allou, juge d'instruction" (Gallimard)

La Bête hurlante (The Howling Beast) 1934
L'Armoire aux poisons (The Poison Cupboard) 1934
Le Collier de sang (The Necklace of Blood) 1934
Le Cri des mouettes (The Seagulls' Cry) 1934
Le Double alibi (The Double Alibi) 1934
Les Masques noirs (Black Masks) 1935
À travers les murailles (Through the Walls) 1937

Collection "La Scarabée d'Or" (Gallimard)

Les Verres noirs (The Black Glasses) 1938

Le Masque (Librarie des Champs-Élysées)

Un mort abusive (An Abusive Death) 1953
Vendredi soir (Friday Night) 1954
La Cinquième Cartouche (The Fifth Cartridge) 1955

*It is ironic, given Vindry's careful differentiation between the adventure novel and the puzzle novel, that his first three puzzle novels were published under Gallimard's rubric "Masterpieces of the Adventure Novel." And that, to this day, the most prestigious French award for mystery stories is called *Le Prix du Roman d'Aventures*. Winners include Boileau, Narcejac and Steeman: also Pierre Véry, André Picot, Peter Lovesey and Paul Halter, all puzzle novel writers.

CHAPTER I

THE STRANGE ATTACK

In October 1919, I was twenty-five years old and had just been appointed deputy magistrate at the court of Aix-en-Provence. I had scarcely become acquainted with my new responsibilities when the examining magistrate, Monsieur Allou, informed me he would be going away for a while and I would be replacing him in his absence.

Who, in Aix, does not remember M. Allou? At first glance there's nothing remarkable about him. Brown-haired, of average height, neither fat nor thin, an oval face, clean-shaven. He could easily go unnoticed; but once he had looked at you, you would never forget those eyes.

In his frank regard you could sense an ability to focus, coupled with a reflective mind, yet with a bold decisiveness that was almost frightening. The contrast with the gentle tones of his deep voice was quite startling.

'My young colleague,' he said, smiling as he spoke, 'you will have the pleasure of standing in for me. I am going on holiday for a couple of weeks.'

And as I protested my inexperience he added, in his slight drawl:

'But you will see, there's nothing to do!'

Indeed M. Allou always gave the impression that he was relaxing. Nonchalantly lounging in an armchair or strolling along the Cours Mirabeau, he seemed to be the laziest judge of the whole court. It was hard to believe that he had a higher case-load than any of his colleagues; he could work hard without giving that impression.

'You'll see,' he insisted, 'there really isn't anything to do. You hear depositions, you read the *Sûreté* reports; and the truth becomes obvious. It's purely routine….'

It certainly appeared that way for him. He had managed to solve several very tricky problems that nobody else would even have understood.

'What ingenuity!' the public prosecutor had said to him once. 'It's lucky you're not a lawbreaker, because nobody would be able to catch you!'

M. Allou left on November 27th at four in the afternoon. And on the morning of Monday the 28th, I replaced him.

In the casual manner of a senior magistrate, I asked as I entered my new chambers:

'Anything new, Monsieur Bonnet?'

And the clerk gave the stock answer, without thinking:

'Nothing new, Your Honour.'

'Or rather, yes!' he added hastily. 'There was a murder yesterday evening.'

I reacted with a start. A murder for my first case! There hadn't been one in Aix for two years, and now one had landed in my lap just as I began my new job.

I asked Bonnet to elaborate. Lifting up his head, so that his greying goatee was no longer hidden behind a pile of papers, my clerk told me:

'We don't know much yet. The *gendarmerie* at Puyricard police phoned this morning. A vagrant has been killed by a young man.'

'Really?' I retorted. 'The world is back to front! It's normally the vagrants that do the killing!'

'Not in Provence, Your Honour. Here, the tramps are usually decent folk...Any way, you'll soon see, Your Honour...A policeman will bring the deposition over and the public prosecutor's office will shortly involve us officially.'

The *gendarme* in question arrived a few minutes later.

'Ah!' he exclaimed. 'It's a strange business. Considering it's the first crime we've ever had in Puyricard, this one's a real beauty. On my word as a *gendarme*!'

Puyricard is a village of some four thousand souls, situated three kilometres from Aix. The inhabitants are indeed peaceful, serious, intelligent and hardworking, like all true natives of Provence—the ones the tourists never see.

'Here's what I can tell you, based on my own initiative and on orders from my superiors,' the *gendarme* continued. 'Yesterday evening, at about six o'clock, a twenty-five year old young man named Pierre Louret, who lives with his father less than a kilometre from the village, was quietly returning home. Three hundred metres from the house he suddenly noticed a tramp, who called out to him: 'You're the Louret son, aren't you?' On receiving a positive response, the tramp suddenly pulled a knife from his pocket and leapt on the young man. But Pierre Louret had readied his revolver as soon as the vagrant started to approach—.'

'So he suspected something,' I remarked. 'But didn't you tell me, Monsieur Bonnet, that the tramps around here are peaceful?'

'This one certainly didn't seem peaceful,' continued the *gendarme*, 'and would have frightened anyone. I have never seen a dirtier beard, nor more disgusting clothes. So, as I was saying, the young man had his revolver at the ready. Dodging the other's charge, he fired his weapon at his attacker, who was killed on the spot.'

'How many bullets?' I asked.

'Supposedly four, Your Honour. Two in the head, two in the heart.'

'Oh!' I observed. 'That's a lot... What determination.'

'It was an automatic pistol,' replied the *gendarme*. 'Once you've fired the first round, it practically continues on its own. But I haven't told you about the strangest part of the business... When we searched the body we found a wallet containing twenty thousand-franc notes.'

'Twenty thousand francs!' I exclaimed.

'Twenty thousand francs. And since the tramp had asked young Louret his name, we concluded he'd been paid to commit a crime...'

I was irritated to hear the *gendarme* refer to "young Louret," who was exactly the same age as I was... So I assumed a more authoritative manner as I continued my questioning.

'Did you know the vagrant?' I asked the *gendarme*.

He informed me the man had appeared in the area eight days ago. As soon as he arrived, he had been asked for his papers; he possessed military identification in the name of Baptiste Florent, had one hundred francs in his pocket, and described himself as an agricultural worker.

And indeed, he had worked in the nearby farms. They appeared happy with him, despite a lack of familiarity with farming, and he was an excellent mechanic. Nobody accused him of pilfering; he didn't hang out in the bars... In fact, he was a model tramp!

Then I questioned the *gendarme* about the Louret family. He didn't know much about them, however, even though they had been in the area for twenty-five years.

The senior Louret had arrived from nobody-knew-where, and built "Cypress Villa." As soon as it was finished, he married a young woman from Marseilles, who bore him two children.

The older child was the Pierre Louret who had killed the vagrant. The other was a girl, Germaine, now twenty-three years old. As for the mother, she had been dead for nearly ten years.

The father and daughter never left the house, so there was probably nobody in the village who could recognise them.

'So who did the shopping?' I asked.

'Their servant, a black American, the same age as his master—fifty-five—and who arrived in the area with him. He's called William, and nobody knows anything more about him; he's never been heard to say a word about anything other than shopping.'

'And what about Mme. Louret, when she was alive?'

'She was only ever seen in the company of her husband.'

'What a strange family, indeed...And doubtless the same goes for the son?'

'Not quite, Your Honour. He went on a number of trips every year; and it was when he was coming back from the railway station that he was attacked.'

'I would like to question him as soon as possible.'

'He expected that, and told me he would come in to see you this morning.'

'Good. Thank you.'

With that, the *gendarme* left.

I telephoned the *Sûreté Générale* immediately. I recommended that fingerprints of the body should be taken at once, in order to determine whether he was already known to the police authorities. And then I waited, at a loss to see what else could be done... I wondered, moreover, whether I had acted too hastily; it had doubtless just been a simple assault...Nevertheless, those twenty thousand francs....

Half an hour later, Pierre Louret arrived. I saw a very tall, very thin young man, dark, with shining, deep-set eyes, and sharp features.

'I am obliged,' I told him, 'to charge you with murder.'

He was clearly startled, and I noticed how nervous he appeared.

'Rest assured,' I continued, 'it's simply a formality and I won't arrest you! As soon as the investigation has established legitimate self-defence, I'll dismiss the case.'

I added that, according to the law, he was not obliged to make any statement in the absence of his lawyer. But he declared that he would not be needing a lawyer and I could ask him any questions I found relevant.

He repeated his account of the incident, from which I learned nothing new.

'Where were you coming from?' I asked him.

'From the station.'

'You had been travelling?'

'Yes, I had left on the 12th of November to spend a couple of weeks with one of my maternal uncles, M. Maurat, who lived in Avignon. He died while I was staying with him.'

'What was the cause of death?'

'A heart attack. He died suddenly on the 20th of November and I stayed on several more days: initially for the funeral, then subsequently for a number of personal matters.'

'Such as?'

'The will. My uncle left everything to my sister and myself.'

'Was there a lot of money involved?'

'More than thirty million francs, according to the executor.'

'And where did he get all that money?'

'In America, where he went with his parents when he was nine years old, and from where he returned about ten years ago.'

'What did he do?'

'I don't know.'

To be honest, I was perfectly aware of the futility of all my questions. But I couldn't think of anything else to ask, and I didn't want to sit silent or still under the somewhat ironic gaze of my clerk. It was important for my first case to be thorough and complete!

So I continued my questioning, somewhat haphazardly. I learned that the parents of the late Maurat had died thirty years ago in America, leaving three children. The oldest, the one who had just died, had stayed a long time in that country and, as I said, only returned to the area recently.

The two others, both girls, returned to France on the death of their parents; they settled in Marseilles at the house of an old aunt, who herself died shortly afterwards.

The younger of the two married M. Louret, father of the young man I was questioning. The other married a Marseilles businessman named Richaud. The couple died in a railway accident eight years ago, leaving a son, Gaston Richaud.

'So you have a first cousin?'

'Yes, he's three years older than I am.'

'Your uncle had a third nephew, then. Why did he disinherit him?'

'I have no idea.'

'Was there bad blood between them?'

'Not at all. My cousin saw my uncle every year.'

I sensed there might be a lead here...The disinherited cousin...revenge against the one who had come into the money....

'Tell me about this Gaston Richaud,' I asked. 'Did you know him?'

'Yes, quite well. He was twenty years old when his parents died and my father took him in for a few months. But he had an independent streak and, in defiance of my father's orders, was out almost every night. I used to let him in each morning; but one day my father found out and there was a terrible scene. As Gaston had inherited a small fortune from his parents, he chose independence and went to live in Lyon, where he studied chemistry. Once he got his diploma, he joined a major pharmaceutical company where, I understand, he is doing very well.'

'Do you see him sometimes?'

'Every year, when I stayed with my uncle in Avignon, I would also go to Lyon and spend a few days with my cousin.'

'You stayed every year with your uncle?'

'Oh! Much more often than that. Two weeks every three months, to be precise.'

Yes, I said to myself, you were cultivating your rich uncle…But I kept that thought to myself.

I continued with my questioning:

'Did your uncle and your cousin ever visit your parents?'

'Never. My uncle never set foot in the place; and my cousin didn't come back after he left, eight years ago.'

'Well,' I said, to bring the questioning to a close, 'that was a frightening experience you had. Being attacked like that, at night…'

'Oh! It wasn't the attack that bothered me…Rather, it was the question he asked beforehand…Why did he ask me if I was Pierre Louret?…And why did a vagrant like that have twenty thousand francs on him?'

His voice was quavering…

'Do you have any enemies?'

'None, I can't think of anyone.'

'And why the life of solitude?'

'It was my father's wish.'

'But your studies?'

'I did them at home with him.'

'If you have no enemies, why do you carry a gun when you go out?'

'Ah! Your Honour,' he replied, 'to understand that, you have to know my family…particularly my father…He seems to live in constant fear of danger, of a hidden menace…It's had a strong influence on me, and I'm never comfortable without a weapon in my pocket…You would only have to spend one evening in our house to understand...Anyway, as things turned out, it was the right thing to do!'

'You seem to believe that your father had enemies,' I observed. 'Could you be more specific?'

'No. He's not a man to share confidences. It's only an impression—but a very strong one.'

'That's enough, thank you. This afternoon I shall hear what your father has to say.'

The young man looked anxious.

'My father…' he murmured…'He really doesn't like to go out….'

'I'm sorry,' I said, 'but the law cannot concern itself with personal tastes!'

And on that note, which seemed to me to be sufficiently weighty, Pierre Louret left.

As he turned to leave, he knocked a chair over. And, once again, I was struck by his nervousness; throughout the questioning, I had noticed frequent awkward gestures.

After he left, I sat deep in thought. This individual appeared to me to be slightly unbalanced; living in such solitude, it was hardly surprising! Wasn't it likely that he would misinterpret a harmless gesture from a vagrant?

However, it was true that a knife had been discovered on the body…Yes, but reaching for the knife could have been a response to the shock of seeing a revolver, and thinking there was a madman involved.

But what about the twenty thousand francs? This family was really so strange…It could have been the vagrant wanting to settle old scores….

No, that seemed hardly likely….

So my thoughts started to follow a different line.

If Pierre Louret died, his father and sister would inherit…And if they in turn died, Gaston Richaud would inherit…victory and revenge at the same time….

I immediately requested Gaston Richaud's file from Lyon with the utmost urgency.

And I waited impatiently for the afternoon. Perhaps I would learn something from Louret senior, possibly an understanding of family matters not known to his children.

Meanwhile, the attack, because of its mysterious nature, caused quite a stir in the town. As I left the Palais de Justice, I was surrounded by journalists coming from Marseilles. In a coldly authoritative tone, I informed them that, for the moment, I had nothing to say to them.

It was, unfortunately, the precise truth…The excellent M. Allou should have stayed on another day!

CHAPTER II

A CURIOUS INDIVIDUAL

At two o'clock, I was back in my chambers and impatiently awaiting M. Louret.

He arrived shortly thereafter.

The man I saw come in was short but wide-shouldered and slightly corpulent, giving an overall impression of forcefulness; the face, which sported a thick grey beard, was of a strange and striking ugliness. The eyes were tiny, the nose broken and twisted, and the skin pitted by smallpox.

It was understandable that he was reluctant to show himself, and one wondered how, even when younger, he had been able to find a wife.

But, more than anything else, I was struck by his air of unease, which he made no attempt to hide, and which was in striking contrast to his apparent vigorous strength.

'It's a bad business,' he said to me, 'a bad business, believe me. Someone was out to get my son, personally….'

'Has he any enemies?'

'No, no, I don't believe so….'

'And what about you, do have any that you know of?'

'No,' he replied hastily, '…No, certainly not! As you must be aware, I don't keep any company.'

'Quite so; so then, why do you believe it was a personal attack?'

'Ah! Your Honour, sometimes families harbour secrets, and it can happen that the children pay for their parents…I never knew mine. I was brought up by an uncle, who died when I was fifteen.'

'How did he die?'

'A heart attack!'

'Goodness, he too,' I exclaimed.

'Yes,' replied Louret, 'it happens fairly frequently between the ages of fifty and sixty.'

'And what did you do after his death?'

'He left me a bit of money and I went to America, where I worked in a number of different businesses. The details are of no importance. I stayed there for fifteen years and came back with a small fortune, which allowed me to make a peaceful retirement for myself in Puyricard.'

I observed that he was only thirty years old at the time, and was rather young to be thinking of retiring....

'Oh! I wasn't at all ambitious,' he replied.

One question still intrigued me: his marriage. If he wasn't particularly rich, how had he found someone willing to marry....

'So you got married?' I asked.

'Yes, a few months after I came back.'

'But you were from Paris originally. How were you able to meet a young lady here so quickly?'

'I had met her father in America.'

'Oh! And what did he do there?'

'He was in business, just like me.'

'And when did he die?'

'Not very long after I came back to France. But may I ask why you want to know all this?'

Up to that point, I hadn't really attached great importance to any of my questions, which I had been asking more or less at random. But Louret's obvious irritation prompted me to persevere.

'You don't need to know,' I replied sharply. 'How old was M. Maurat senior when he died?'

'I don't know exactly...Fifty or sixty years old, maybe.'

'Well! Fifty or sixty years old...And did he die, as his son did on the 20th of November last, of a heart attack?'

I had spoken off the cuff. The curtness of the reply was noticeable:

'I have no idea. We didn't live in the same place. He lived in Chicago and I had been in New York.'

'So how did you know each other? Did you go to Chicago from time to time?'

'No, I never set foot there. But he sometimes came to New York.'

Louret's replies were becoming almost aggressive. I had been about to comment, but it occurred to me that what I was interpreting as anger may well just have been fear. Truly, the man appeared very uneasy...Was it my questions or the bad memories they invoked?

For several moments I said nothing.

'Look,' I continued, 'if you feel you're in danger, it would be better to tell me the truth. Don't you suspect anything?...Your American friends...your family....'

'Nothing...nothing...' he murmured.

'At Puyricard you never went out; why?'

‘I don’t like people. And anyway,’ he added angrily, ‘do you think I like walking around with a face like mine?’

I promised him the most absolute secrecy, but to no avail: I couldn’t get anything more out of him.

He had barely left my chambers when I heard the sound of an explosion, followed by a howl of terror…I recognised Louret’s voice and rushed out in alarm.

But no sooner was I outside than I burst out laughing. The noise had come from a news photographer’s flashbulb. And I assumed that Louret, realising it was a false alarm, would be laughing as well.

Not a bit of it. Fear was still written all over his face; but now it was mixed with unbridled fury.

‘I forbid you…’ he stammered…‘I forbid you to publish my photograph.’

But, without stopping to answer, the photographers ran off with their prize. I feared he might try to attack them, and placed a restraining hand on his arm.

‘Calm down,’ I said, ‘it’s nothing. You seem a little upset today.’

‘I have good reason!’

‘I realise it’s been a strange experience. I very much regret that my colleague, M. Allou, is not here. He has a knack of sorting out the trickiest situations.’

‘And when’s he coming back?’ asked Louret brusquely.

I found the question rather offensive; one is always irked to find one’s modesty taken seriously….

‘Two weeks from now,’ I replied tersely. And, with these words, I left him.

The following morning (Tuesday 29th of November), on opening my newspaper, I saw the photographs of M. Louret and his son. The former was a particularly striking resemblance, perfectly capturing his tough yet furtive look.

Around ten o’clock, I was paid two strange visits.

The first was from a reputable Aix businessman, M. René Massot. He was a man of average height and corpulence, with a remarkably young face, despite his grey hair and white moustache.

He asked that we might talk on a strictly private basis; my clerk excused himself without further ado.

M. Massot first asked for my vow of complete confidence regarding what he was about to say. Then he added:

‘I thought my testimony might be useful. Thirty years ago, I was living in America, and in fact met M. Louret there.’

'In New York?' I asked.

'No, Your Honour, in Chicago.'

'In Chicago? Are you quite sure?'

'It's the only American city I've ever been to.'

'That's strange,' I murmured…'He swore to the contrary…And you say he lived there?'

'Yes, but under another name, which I have forgotten.'

'How can you be sure it was M. Louret?'

'Because I recognised his photograph in the morning paper.'

'Just a minute!' I replied. 'A man can change in thirty years.…'

'Your Honour, I'm sure you've noticed that Louret's ugliness is quite out of the ordinary. Once seen, never forgotten; and the same goes for his stare. He's grown a beard, but nothing short of a mask could ever prevent him being recognised.'

'And you met him often in Chicago?'

'Probably a dozen times.'

'Was he one of your friends?'

'Oh no, Your Honour!' exclaimed Massot. 'He was not the sort you want to be friends with!'

'Why so?'

'He was mixed up in some ugly business.'

'What kind of business?'

'I can't be specific…It was just a reputation he had; but sufficiently well-established that honest businessmen didn't want to deal with him…He was rumoured to be part of organised crime.'

'But wasn't he ever arrested?'

'Never, to my knowledge.'

'Fair enough,' I said, getting up, 'I'll arrange a meeting between the two of you.'

René Massot went pale. He leant forward and said, in a low voice:

'I warn you I shall not repeat my allegations in front of him. He's a dreadful human being. Over there, they said he would stop at nothing. Remember your promise of secrecy.'

'Understood,' I replied. 'For that matter, your statement does not have any direct bearing on the case under review. Nevertheless, I thank you for your information.'

M. Massot departed, leaving me perplexed.…

Shortly thereafter, there was a fresh knock on the door of my chambers. And into the room came a stunningly pretty woman. But her garish clothes, heavy make-up, and a certain something in her expression left no doubt as to her profession.

'My name is Rose Pompon,' she told me.
'Is that your real name, madam?'
'Yes, Your Honour....'
'What I mean is: is that the name you were given at birth?'
'That's to say...my real name is Adelaide Godillot. But everybody knows me as Rose Pompon.'
'I must say, it suits you much better,' I observed. 'And what is the purpose of your visit?'
'Well, Your Honour, what I have to say is of no importance, but I thought it might be important all the same. Do you see what I mean?'
'Not very well; but please continue.'
'It's just that...those in my profession are often suspect; it's not fair, but that's the way it is. So I thought it'd be best if I made the first move and came in and told you everything I know, even though I don't know anything.'
'You did the right thing; so now tell me everything you don't know...'
'No, Your Honour. I'm going to tell you what I know, and only what I know...So...This morning I recognised M. Louret's photograph in the newspaper.'
I sat up, startled.
'And how did you know him?' I enquired.
Rose Pompon lowered her eyes with a becoming modesty.
'I was his mistress for six months,' she replied.
'Be specific.'
And, with the same affected airs which she hoped in vain sounded respectable, the lovely young thing continued:
'We stopped seeing each other exactly one month ago today. I met him in the beginning of May.'
'Where was that?'
'In Marseilles.'
'So he went to Marseilles?'
'Yes, Your Honour, regularly. Two afternoons a week.'
'Well, well!... And what caused the break-up?'
Rose Pompon's expression was even more coy than before.
'He didn't have any more money, Your Honour,' she murmured, with a timid smile.
'Yes,' I observed, 'at least that's what he told you.'
She sat up haughtily like a woman whose honour had been impugned.

'What are you insinuating?' she retorted. 'That he'd had enough of me? I'll have you know that he begged me at first, then threatened me! Yes, Your Honour, threatened me; he said he'd kill me and then kill himself afterwards…And if he'd said the same to you in the same tone, magistrate or not, you'd have been as scared as I was!'

'I can't conceive of any circumstance in which he would have said that,' I replied drily. 'Nevertheless, continue. You didn't give in?'

Rose Pompon's face wore an expression of modesty once again.

'Put yourself in my place, Your Honour…He's so ugly...But even though I'm used to that kind of scene, I can assure you I was really scared!'

'In any case he recanted, luckily.…'

'I beg your pardon?'

'I meant to say: he changed his mind and didn't kill you.…'

'No; all of a sudden he said to me: I'll come back with the money. At the time, I was pretty pleased; but now, with all that's happened, I'm not so sure…after all…you understand…I wouldn't want anyone to think…Nobody's ever said anything bad about me, Your Honour!'

'There's one thing I find surprising,' I commented. 'M. Louret had come back from America with a small fortune.…'

'Well,' sighed Rose Pompon, 'he didn't spend it all on me! For twenty years, I've been told, he's had all the best-looking girls of Marseilles. With a face like his, that must have cost him a fortune!'

'Quite,' I agreed, in spite of myself. 'One last question, mademoiselle. Did you go out together to shows, or to restaurants…?'

'Never, Your Honour; in fact it was quite tiresome. He had rented a room in the suburbs, and I used to meet him there.'

'Did you know his name?'

'He told me he was called Durand, but I never believed him. It was such a common name, it couldn't be true. By the way, he'd said the same to Laure, the girl he was seeing before he met me.'

As a precaution, I dictated the deposition to my clerk, and dismissed the lovely young person.

That afternoon, M. Louret reappeared without warning. If he had appeared uneasy the day before, today he appeared terrified. His features were distorted; he stammered, unable to complete a single sentence.

'We're finished,' he repeated incessantly, 'we're finished.…'

And, with a trembling hand, he proffered a letter:

'I found it…no stamp…in the letter-box, a short while ago.…'

I took the letter and noted that somebody had cut out letters from a newspaper, to form the following words:

"This time we've found you and we won't let you go. It's time to settle accounts. The children will avenge the parents. You and yours are condemned to die."

Needless to say, there was no signature.

While I was reading the letter, Louret kept moaning:

'My children…my children…protect my children!'

'Monsieur,' I said sternly, if you want to be protected, you must first tell me the truth. Now, I happen to know that you have already lied to me twice….'

'No… no!'

'Yes! First of all, you did live in Chicago. Secondly, you had until quite recently a mistress in Marseilles, whom you visited twice a week!'

He seemed to collapse, and stammered a few words of confession. If he were to be believed, he had concealed his private life because he did not want his children to read about their father's behaviour in the newspaper. As far as his time in Chicago, he was guilty of a few indiscretions (oh! but nothing serious…), but now he wanted to bury the past…

'You're not telling me everything,' I said, taking a guess. 'If you want to save your skin, you'd better confess everything; you're obviously scared of vengeance. So you'd better talk; we'll find out pretty soon anyway!'

For a few seconds, he appeared to hesitate.

'No, no…' he said at last, 'that's all…I've told you everything.'

'But how do you explain why the writer of the letter is out for revenge?'

'It's a mistake, a terrible mistake…A physical resemblance perhaps, or a similar name....'

'A resemblance,' I said. 'Your photograph did in fact appear this morning…A resemblance…that would be very strange….'

I realised the cruelty of my words as soon as I had spoken them.

'You mean there can't be two men so ugly?' exclaimed Louret. 'I had a brother, Your Honour!'

'And what happened to him?'

'I don't know. I lost contact with him once I left for America.'

'We can't do anything for you,' I said, rising from my chair. 'Do the best you can…Why not go and hide in some other region?'

'No…no…They'll follow us…At home, at least, I know where I am...I feel safe behind closed doors.'

And with these words he left.

To be on the safe side, I had his papers verified by Paris, and learned later that they were in order.

CHAPTER III

THINGS GET WORSE

The next day, Wednesday the 30th of November, I was in my chambers by eight o'clock, anticipating new developments in the case.

I went through the mail. There was a police report on the incident involving the vagrant. The investigation had yielded nothing new. Nobody had seen the victim talking to the suspect. And the inspector in charge of the case saw no point in continuing any further, at least until there had been a response from Paris concerning the fingerprints.

But, at half past eight, the phone rang. The Puyricard *gendarmerie* informed me that, during the night, there had been an attempted break-in at Cypress Villa, the home of M. Louret.

I decided to go there immediately. The public prosecutor had just arrived; accompanied by my clerk, we hailed a taxi and found ourselves thirty minutes later in front of the house which was about to achieve a tragic notoriety.

As I said before, it was less than a mile from the village. Access was initially via a little-used narrow road, then a dirt track which we had to follow for about three hundred metres before discovering the villa. I say "discovering" because it was located behind a small hill which hid it from the road. We would never have found it if one of the village peasants had not accompanied us.

The house was of medium size and totally lacking in style, even though good quality material appeared to have been used in its construction.

The first thing which struck us when we arrived was that all the shutters were closed. It was as if preparations had been made for a siege! And the black servant only opened the door for us after calling his master, who recognised my voice through the door.

I found the whole family assembled in the lounge. The room was lit by a petrol-lamp. And M. Louret flatly refused to open the shutters.

He appeared, if that were possible, to be even more distressed than the previous day. Slumped in an armchair, he barely heard the questions, which had to be repeated two or three times.

As for his son, Pierre Louret, the nervousness I had noticed before had become distinctly more pronounced, and was troubling to watch.

With his long stride, he paced up and down the room and succeeded in bumping into every one of the few pieces of furniture.

I had immediately been struck, not only by the poor taste, but also by the poor quality of the furniture, which had been reduced to the absolute bare minimum. And there was not a single item of value to be seen: the distant influence of Rose Pompon and her friends could be felt.

But I was most struck by Germaine Louret. She bore a strong resemblance to her brother. Tall, pale, with a long face, she couldn't be called ugly; on the contrary she had quite regular features. But there was something distant in her gaze which discouraged familiarity. It didn't take long for me to realise, from her words and gestures, that she was as nervous as her brother.

She described to me, in clipped phrases, the events of the previous night.

Around one o'clock in the morning, she had been awakened by a strange sound. She soon realised that someone was trying to force open the shutters of her room. She shouted at the top of her voice, and shortly thereafter heard her father and brother knocking at her door. She drew the bolts and they came into the room.

I asked her why she had not run into the corridor immediately.

'I was afraid there might be someone out there as well. That's why I only opened the door when I heard the voices of my family...Ah! What a terrible experience...I almost fainted, and I still don't know how I avoided it!'

'She's very excitable,' confirmed M. Louret.

I went outside to look at the shutter. There were indeed obvious signs of forced entry—caused, no doubt, by pliers. Afterwards, I walked through the house.

Here's the description.

There were two storeys.

There were five windows in the south-facing wall of the ground floor, corresponding, from east to west, to the rooms as follows:

The first was in the stairwell, and extended upwards to the first floor. Solid iron bars prevented any entry from this direction.

The second and third windows were in the lounge where we had been received, which also served as a dining-room.

The fourth was in one of the bedrooms—in fact the daughter's—and was where the attempted break-in had occurred.

The fifth was in another bedroom, this one occupied by M. Louret.

The front (and only) door was in the east façade. Leading from it was a corridor going east-west, with the three rooms mentioned above giving on to it. Walking down it, one found in turn on one's left: first the stairwell, slightly recessed relative to the interior wall of the corridor; then the lounge; Germaine Louret's bedroom; and M. Louret's bedroom at the end.

Even so, the corridor did not extend to the west façade of the house. It was blocked by a partition, behind which lay a small kitchen, accessed by a door in the partition almost exactly opposite the front door.

In the north wall, on the right of the corridor, there were no rooms and just two windows.

Finally, on the west façade was the only window of the kitchen.

The first floor had exactly the same layout as the ground floor, except for a window in the east façade over the front door.

Pierre Louret slept up there in the room over his sister's; and so, too, did William, whose room was over the kitchen. The two other rooms were unoccupied and entirely unfurnished.

Finally, in the ceiling of the first floor corridor, towards the head of the stairs, was a trap door giving access to the attic. It was kept shut by two enormous bolts and an equally large padlock.

Naturally, I insisted on visiting the attic. It had a very low ceiling: about five feet at its highest point. One part had been organised as a pigeon-loft, with several small openings around the edge of the roof.

Two things struck me during the visit to the house.

First, the paucity of the furniture. Second, the solidity of the construction and of the doors and windows.

Each room, whether on the ground floor or the first, was separated, be it from its neighbour or from the corridor, by a masonry wall thirty centimetres thick; only the kitchen and William's room were separated from the corridor by a single layer of bricks.

Similarly, on each floor the shutters were extremely solid, being made of iron and covered with such a profusion of hooks and bars that opening any one of them would take at least a minute. I felt, therefore, that any attempt at entry was obviously doomed to failure and the fear of the inhabitants in that regard was not justified.

The door to each room, likewise, was as solid as the shutters. Extremely thick, each one was locked by two enormous bolts, one on top and one on the bottom, not accessible from the outside. And, as for the front door, I shan't even bother describing it.

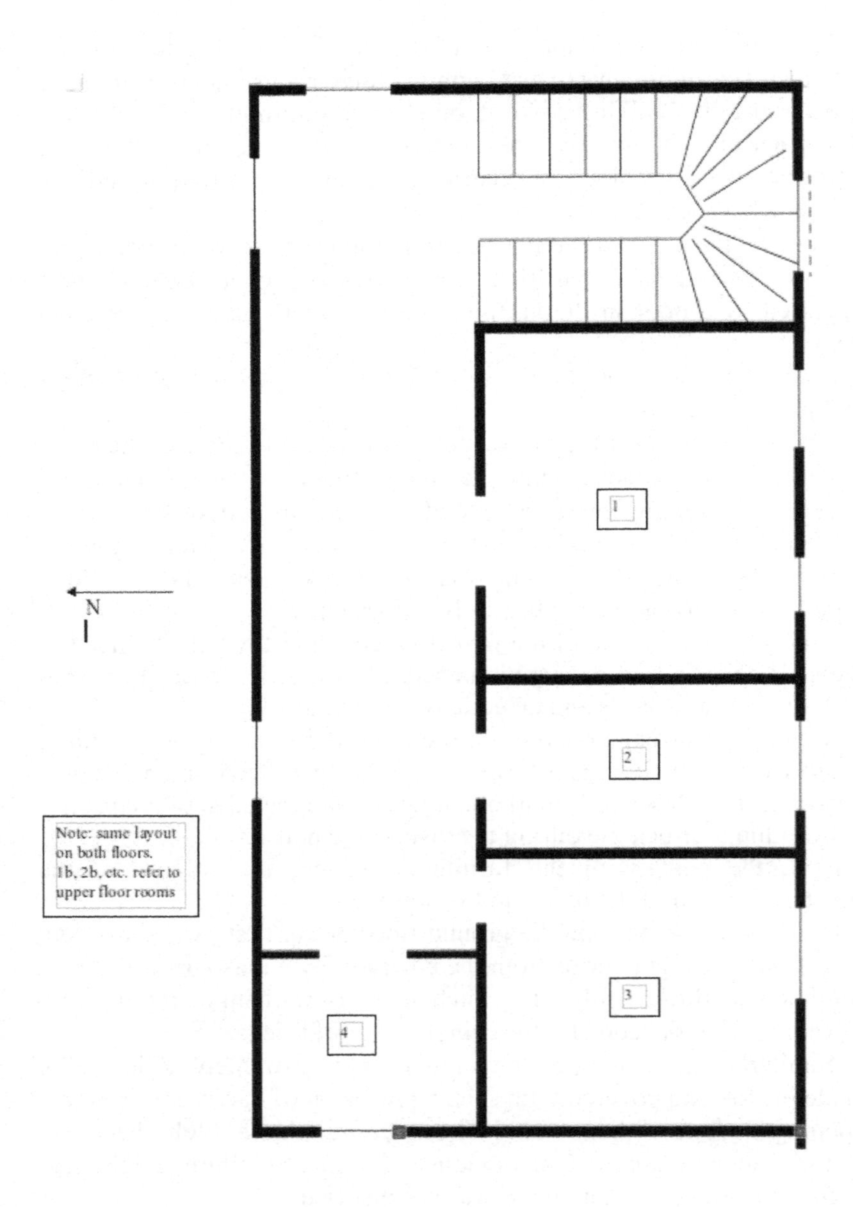
1
2
3
4
N
Note: same layout on both floors. 1b, 2b, etc. refer to upper floor rooms

To be truthful, I was surprised that only the stairwell window was barred. But M. Louret explained to me that that mode of protection was very dangerous in case of fire, and solid shutters were just as effective.

To complete my inspection, I must record that there was not one single chimney in the house, except for a simple tubular pipe for the kitchen stove. Heating was provided by oil-fired stoves.

There was no cellar, which was easy to verify, given that there were no carpets in the rooms; there was in fact a thick one, which I lifted up, in the ground floor corridor.

Finally, there were no communicating doors between any of the rooms.

At the end of the visit, I drew up a plan of the house, which I reproduce here. I have numbered the rooms 1 to 4, starting from the front door, 4 being the kitchen. From now on, I shall refer to each room by its number. For the upper floor, I shall use 1b, 2b, etc…because the layout is identical to the lower one.

Once the inspection was complete, we found ourselves in the lounge (no. 1). Pierre Louret had resumed his clumsy walk; and I suddenly noticed that everyone was looking at me…I was, in effect, the leader of the expedition, and it was up to me to decide; yes, but decide what? The futility of this trip to the house was becoming painfully obvious to me.

To cover my confusion and prepare for an honourable retreat, I adopted a serious tone and requested more details, no doubt useless.

'I have heard your daughter's statement,' I said to Louret. 'Now I would like to know exactly what you yourself saw and heard.'

Louret looked up and, in a slightly breathless voice, told me:

'I was wakened by Germaine's cries, terrible cries…I rushed straight out into the corridor, where I found my son, who had also heard them….'

I told myself that Louret was embellishing his own role and covering up the fear that had momentarily paralysed him. He had apparently found his son in the corridor; now, Pierre Louret was sleeping on the floor above; in order to go downstairs he would have had to cover half of the first floor corridor, then the stairs. How could he have arrived first at his sister's room if the father had indeed left his own room immediately?

I presumed that panic had frozen him in his footsteps. But he again insisted that he had gone from his bed to the corridor in one bound;

nevertheless, I did not believe him, vividly recalling his pitiful display in my chambers the day before.

'Your room is immediately adjacent to your daughter's,' I pointed out. 'Did you really not hear any noise at all from the attempted entry?'

'Absolutely nothing. I'm a very heavy sleeper, by the way.'

'And you, monsieur,' I said, turning to Pierre Louret. 'You were in the room immediately above your sister's: didn't you hear anything at all unusual?'

No, he too had only been alerted by his sister's cries. Likewise William, who had rushed downstairs to arrive only a few moments after the others.

It was the turn of the servant to be interrogated. He reaffirmed his statement, explaining that when he arrived downstairs, the girl had already opened her door and "de massas was already inside." Standing in the doorway, he had been struck by Germaine Louret's pallor.

'Someone had found time to light a lamp?' I asked.

'I always sleep with a strong nightlight,' the girl replied.

'In that case, mademoiselle, it was a mistake not to extinguish it as soon as you heard the first noise.'

'Of course,' exclaimed her father. 'If you stay in the light against an invisible attacker, you present a perfect target and you are completely defenceless. On the other hand, if you stay completely motionless in the dark, you force the attacker to betray his own position by his movements, and he's the one that becomes the target!'

'Alas, Your Honour,' chimed in Pierre Louret, 'my sister has no *sang-froid*. Yesterday, after my father received the famous letter, I advised her several times to take that basic precaution!'

The young woman promised that, from now on, she wouldn't forget.

'You were armed, of course?' I asked her.

'Yes, I always have my revolver ready to hand.'

I rose to leave. M. Louret accompanied me to the door and opened the letter-box.

He gave a startled cry: there was an envelope lying there. With a trembling hand, he withdrew it and removed a sheet of paper, which he read before handing to me. I saw, in printed letters, the following words:

WE FAILED LAST NIGHT. WE WILL TRY AGAIN TONIGHT

'Well, now, this is curious,' I remarked. 'Normally, would-be murderers are not so obliging as to notify their victims in advance!'

'Don't forget,' said the public prosecutor, 'that we're dealing with revenge. Death is but an instant. But the agony that precedes it is far more terrible. That's true revenge!'

It was enough to look at M. Louret to recognise the wisdom of that observation…Suddenly, he was on his knees before me:

'Don't leave us alone,' he cried. 'Give us some protection, or we're finished!'

I observed that the house appeared impregnable. But nothing would reassure him.

'All right,' I said at last. 'I'll ask the Aix police commissioner to send a local police inspector here tonight, to help you guard the house….'

'Just one?' asked Pierre Louret in turn. 'Don't you think there should be at least two, one inside the house and one on guard outside?'

'I beg you,' added the young woman.

I was touched, and promised that an inspector would come, with two *gendarmes* to stand guard over the approach roads. I observed, as I was leaving, that it would be easy work. There was an uninterrupted view for several hundred yards in every direction; the small hill which hid the house from the road had a very gentle slope. There were only two trees in the surrounding area: two cypresses, quite far from the villa, and too thin for even a child to hide behind.

Nothing was going to happen to them that night, I thought as I left. But we could not continue to supply them with a three-man bodyguard indefinitely!

CHAPTER IV

THE FANTASTIC CRIME

On my return to my chambers, around two o'clock, I contacted the police commissioner and explained the situation to him. He deemed it to be quite dangerous.

I pointed out that we couldn't send in an army, all the same! Particularly since we might be the victims of a practical joke; or of a simple attempt at blackmail.

The commissioner agreed. However, he added that he would first ask for volunteers, and only if there were none would he resort to designating personnel.

His call to the inspectors turned out to be fruitful. There were five immediate volunteers. He chose a certain Clement, who was very persistent and claimed he had not been given an interesting assignment in five years. 'You've all had something,' he said to his colleagues. 'Now it's my turn to be in the limelight.'

This Clement was fat and stocky, with a florid face embellished—if that's the word—with an enormous red moustache. Although in the Aix "secret police" for five years, and well-regarded, he had not yet distinguished himself in any way.

As for the *gendarmes*, their captain chose Jean Vaneau first, on the grounds of having the best vision of the squad, being able to see at night like a cat. With him was Gendarme Roustan, noted for his gifts of observation and the accuracy of his reports.

Inspector Clement and the two officers, all heavily armed, left for Cypress Villa. And here, from what I learnt the following day, is how events unfolded.

The three men arrived at four o'clock. And their first task was to verify the security of all the doors and windows. That done, it was agreed that Gendarme Vaneau—he of the exceptional vision—would be stationed outside, in order to survey all the approaches; he noted that the visibility was perfect.

'But nevertheless,' he pointed out, 'I cannot see both front and back simultaneously.'

The inspector pointed out that he would only be expected to patrol outside the house, which was not very big. It would not be possible, given the wide field of vision, for anyone to enter or leave one side of the house while the officer was on the other side, provided he did not stop on his rounds.

'Well,' said Vaneau, smiling, 'it looks as though I'll be walking several kilometres tonight. Luckily, I'm used to it!'

'What's more,' added the inspector, 'I'll help you with the surveillance. I shall be based in the upstairs corridor, next door to the stairwell. I'm going to leave the shutters of the two windows next to me open, so that I'll have a continuous view to the east and the north.'

'That's an excellent idea,' observed Pierre Louret. 'As for me, as I have no intention of sleeping, I shall watch from my window, so that the southern aspect will be covered.'

'What are you thinking of?' exclaimed his father. 'Leaving your shutters open…!'

'The window is high up,' replied the young man, 'and can't be reached without a ladder. And it wouldn't be possible for someone to bring a ladder without M. Vaneau or myself seeing them, for heaven's sake. And even though a shutter takes time to secure properly, it can be shut very quickly. I'll turn all the lights out in my room, of course.'

M. Louret admired the courage of his son, but made no attempt to imitate him. In any case, his surveillance would have been redundant.

On the other hand, William, whose window opened to the west, proposed that he also watch. His offer was accepted.

Then the besieged, if I may call them that, realised that it would be madness, given the circumstances, to stay scattered throughout the house. It was agreed that everyone would be based on the first floor.

They moved the beds, or more accurately the mattresses and blankets; for Germaine Louret had a horror of beds, beneath which, according to her, one always had the impression someone was lurking.

Her father agreed with her observation and did the same. He decided to take the room above the lounge, immediately adjacent to the head of the stairs (1b).

Pierre Louret kept his (2b).

Finally, Germaine Louret took room 3b, whose walls adjoined those of her brother, to the east, and William, to the north.

'As for me,' announced the inspector, 'I shall, as I said, place a chair in the corridor at the head of the stairs. I shall be able to see, at the same time, two windows—at the north and the east; the trapdoor to the attic, which will be over my head; and the stairs.'

I forgot to mention that the inspector had brought a dozen oil lamps. He lit them and placed them around the house, in addition to those already there, thus illuminating all the dark corners.

Germaine Louret asked for a table in her room. Inspector Clement only allowed her a very small one and one chair; he pointed out that it was too easy to hide in a room, so the less furniture the better.

The young woman went pale at the thought of all the detailed precautions, which underlined the danger they were facing.

Gendarme Vaneau dined before the others and left to take up his post. As for Clement, he announced he was not going to eat; he would not even accept a glass of wine.

The meal passed without incident. Then, accompanied by Clement, who had just completed yet another tour to check security, the Lourets went into the lounge, while *gendarme* Roustan patrolled the corridors.

The evening was pretty dismal. Neither M. Louret nor his daughter said a word. Pierre Louret started and gasped at the slightest scrape of the furniture, which did little to calm the nerves of his companions; to the point that, on several occasions, Germaine Louret appeared on the point of fainting.

Outside, one could hear owls hooting.

'I don't like those awful creatures,' commented Clement. 'Is it like that every night?'

'Every night,' replied M. Louret, in a lugubrious voice.

Clement tried to cheer everyone up with his patter, without success.

'It would be better if we went to our rooms and observation posts now,' he announced shortly thereafter.

The atmosphere was indeed becoming uncomfortable. Everyone stood up to go upstairs. It was ten o'clock.

'We're going to check the security once more,' declared Clement. 'Will everybody please stay close to me while this is being done.'

The inspection tour started in the kitchen, where they found William, who joined the group.

A close examination revealed nothing unusual on the ground floor; the group went upstairs, where everyone then shut themselves in their room. Only Gendarme Roustan stayed downstairs, where he was careful to open all the interior doors. The inspector went to sit on his chair, after having carefully opened the shutters of the two windows as planned, but leaving the windows themselves shut because of the cold. Having done that, he spotted Gendarme Vaneau doing his rounds.

'Anything to report?' he asked.

'Nothing,' came the reply.

'It's a mistake to close the windows,' Pierre Louret told Clement. 'If anything happens outside, you won't hear it as clearly.'

'It's cold,' murmured the inspector.

'That's not good enough,' retorted the young man. 'I'll lend you my coat, which is very thick. I have a large dressing gown for myself, which reaches to my toes. William has a very good overcoat. Under those circumstances, why close the windows?'

So they decided to leave the windows open wherever anyone was watching.

And silence descended on the villa, broken only by the occasional hooting of the owls. The light of the moon was so strong that Vaneau could see as clearly as in daylight.

One hour passed...Then another...And what happened after that was confirmed unanimously by all the witnesses.

At around one o'clock, anguished cries were heard coming from the young woman's room. A few seconds later, from the same room, three revolver shots rang out. Then came the sound of a body falling to the floor.

At the same time that the shots were ringing out, Pierre Louret rushed out of his room and into the corridor, emitting a terrible cry. Less than a second later, M. Louret and the servant William also came out. In front of Germaine Louret's door they met Inspector Clement, who shouted: "Open up! Open up!"

At the same time Roustan appeared, having climbed the stairs in practically a single bound.

But the bedroom door appeared firmly bolted on the inside. 'Break it down!' shouted Pierre Louret. As one, the five men flung themselves at the door, M. Louret on the side of the hinge, the officer on the side of the lock. But, as I said before, the bolts in that house were very solid and only broke at the fourth attempt.

The bolt at the top gave way first; and, in the opening, Roustan, who was the closest, could see that the lower bolt was still in place. But there was not enough room to pass his hand; it required another push before it, too, gave way.

From the doorway, a horrifying sight stopped everyone in their tracks. The lamp in the room was out; but the brilliantly illuminated corridor gave out a diffuse light. In the middle of the room lay the body of the young woman, parallel to the window.

Then the inspector said: 'Follow me!'

A quick look round the room showed it to be empty, apart from the body. With one swift movement, the inspector had seized the mattress and turned it over: there was nobody hidden in the bed or behind the door.

In the same second, all eyes went to the window. It was shut, and it was obvious that the shutters were closed tight and absolutely intact.

'It's fantastic,' murmured Clement. And he went over to the young woman and knelt down, leaning over her, and lifted her head.

M. Louret had sat down heavily on the bed, without uttering a word.

William stood motionless in the doorway next to the *gendarme*, who continued to watch the corridor....

As for Pierre Louret, he was completely unable to contain himself, shrieking hideously: 'Germaine! Germaine!' He approached the body, which Clement was still holding.

'Look,' he said suddenly, 'there's blood!'

And indeed, a dark liquid was spreading slowly from the body, at the level of the breast, and was oozing in the direction of the door. The inspector dipped his finger in it, and brought it up to his face. There could be no doubt about the odour: it was blood.

'There's been a crime, there's no doubt,' he announced, placing the body back on the floor.

'Maybe she's not dead,' shouted Pierre Louret. 'Light the lamp!'

And, at the same time, on his knees, he raised the body of his sister, which Clement had put down. He clutched it to himself, shouting:

'Germaine! Germaine! Answer me! You're not dead, tell me you're not dead....'

Meanwhile, the inspector had struck a match and lit the lamp, and now approached the body again.

'Leave her,' he told Pierre Louret. 'We'll examine her.'

The other gently put his sister back on the floor. But suddenly he shouted:

'The knife...there...look...the knife.'

And, in the clear light of the lamp, a tiny handle could be seen near the left breast. With a swift movement, Pierre Louret pulled the weapon out: it was a small triangular dagger.

'Ah!' he moaned. 'Stabbed in the heart. The bastards...They've killed her...They've killed her....'

The inspector put the lamp down, leant over, and examined the evidence. Germaine Louret was now a corpse.

Everyone stood there, stunned. Pierre Louret was sobbing quietly. And suddenly, it was the father, his face buried in the bolster, who was shouting:

'My daughter…my daughter…Germaine! They've killed my daughter!'

'Nevertheless,' said Clement, 'you've all been witnesses, the room was locked and there was nobody inside….'

Everyone nodded.

'So…' continued Clement, 'so…it's suicide….'

'No,' shouted the father. 'I can swear she didn't possess a dagger.'

'It's true,' confirmed Pierre Louret and William simultaneously.

Besides, people were starting to recall that, from the doorway of the room, the young woman's right hand could clearly be seen still clutching her revolver, while the left hand clutched the back of the chair which the victim had overturned while falling.

It was obvious, therefore, that she couldn't have stabbed herself with her left hand. And, if she had wanted to kill herself, she would surely have used the revolver, which would have taken less effort.

'Don't touch anything in this room,' ordered Inspector Clement. 'Roustan, look out of the nearest open window and see what's happened to your fellow officer.'

The *gendarme* was soon back: Vaneau had not seen anything. He had been on the other side of the house when he had heard Germaine Louret screaming; he had rushed round in front of her window and had heard the revolver shots, but had seen absolutely nothing.

The inspector went over to the shutters, to inspect the fastenings more closely. Everything was as it should be.

'Stay here,' he said to the four men. I'm going to check all the windows in the house again.'

He returned a short while later, crestfallen….

'Nothing's out of place,' he muttered, 'nothing's out of place…it's truly diabolical…unless it's a ghost….'

At that pronouncement, it appeared that William would faint, especially as the *gendarme* could be heard murmuring: 'It's been known to happen…it's been known….'

All night long, they watched over the body. Outside, Vaneau continued his rounds. But day broke without anything further happening.

'William,' said the inspector, 'go to the police station and alert them.'

I was notified at eight o'clock, as I arrived in my chambers. Once more accompanied by the public prosecutor and my clerk, I quickly found a taxi.

'I read about something similar in the case of "The Mystery of the Yellow Room",' the prosecutor told me.

'And what was the explanation?'

'The young woman had been struck, but not fatally. After her attacker had gone, she had automatically shot the bolts before fainting. When she came to, she called for help and, hallucinating, she fired a number of rounds from her revolver. When the door was forced open, needless to say, there was no sign of an assailant in the room.'

I pointed out to the prosecutor that such an explanation did not apply in our case. First of all, the assailant could not have entered or left at any time, because Clement had been in front of the door; afterwards, even supposing the young woman had been complicit in some way, she would have cried out once she was attacked; finally, with a dagger plunged into her heart, she could hardly have gone around shooting the bolts and locking herself in again.

We arrived at Cypress Villa. The flying squad, called in by the local police, was already on the spot, and Chief Superintendent Dumas, head of the *Sûreté,* came to greet us; I had recognised this peaceful giant from his silhouette as we arrived.

'Ah!' I exclaimed, 'if what I was told on the phone is accurate, we are face to face with the most extraordinary crime ever known!'

Dumas shrugged his shoulders.

'There's no mystery! There's a trapdoor, for heaven's sake!'

'Did you find it?' I asked.

'Not yet, but we're looking.'

They looked for it all day, with no success. The walls, though thick, could not have concealed a passage wide enough for even a child. Nonetheless, they were examined with great care, as were the ceilings and floors. Five flying squad officers were involved in the search.

'Everything must be examined in the finest detail,' I said. 'Any hole, even the size of a pinprick, could be important.'

I went upstairs. While one man inspected the ceiling, another was wielding a pick-axe to smash the tiling. I heard a third man in the attic, obviously busy examining the ceiling from that side. The other two men were examining the walls an inch at a time, one behind the other, each with a magnifying-glass, so that every spot was inspected twice.

An experiment was tried, involving gas. The attic, the lounge, William's room, and Pierre Louret's were pumped full of vapours with a distinctive smell, one molecule of which being immediately detectable in a room, even by someone with a poor sense of smell. Thus, the slightest pin-hole could be detected.

The test yielded no results. Nothing penetrated the room of the crime, unless it wafted in much later, from the corridor.

And the various drillings led nowhere either....

I asked the head of the *Sûreté* if he had any theories.

'Maybe...' he replied. 'William, the servant, has gone missing.'

'What?'

'This morning, he went to notify the local *gendarmerie*, but he hasn't been seen since.'

'Perhaps he's been killed as well,' I murmured...

At that very moment, a peasant appeared. He had come to tell us that, a quarter of an hour ago, he had seen the black manservant—easily recognisable, even from afar—hiding in a copse.

'It's strange that he didn't go farther afield,' I observed.

'He knows that all the roads are under observation,' replied Dumas.

'They weren't this morning, early on,' I retorted.

'That's true,' conceded the chief superintendent. 'In any case, the *gendarmes* are sweeping the countryside, so it won't be long before they bring him in.'

'That's strange...very strange...' I murmured.

'There's something even stranger,' continued Dumas.

'Of course,' I replied, thinking of the actual crime.

'There's something you don't know about yet. According to all the witnesses, three shots were fired. What's more, there are three empty cartridges in the young woman's revolver. Now, listen carefully, we have only found two bullets!'

'Whereabouts?'

'In the wall, to the right of the window...And, bearing in mind the intense scrutiny, even the slightest trace of the third bullet would have been detected! So it means that someone was hit....'

'Maybe we'll find it in the victim's own body!' I suggested.

But the medical examiner, who arrived shortly thereafter, determined that my hunch was wrong. After a thorough examination, the young woman's body revealed nothing more than the fatal stab wound.

'It was straight to the heart,' the examiner said, 'and death must have been instantaneous.'

'Don't you think it could have been suicide?'

'No. From the direction of the thrust, there's no possibility of that whatsoever.'

I spent several more hours interrogating the witnesses. I learnt nothing more than what I have already related.

However, I did learn from Clement that, a few moments before the crime, he had heard a slight noise coming from the young woman's room, like a gentle tapping on wood. But he had barely had time to think about it when the screams occurred, followed by the revolver shots.

'Why didn't you eat?' I asked him.

'Because, Your Honour, I ate some provisions I brought myself. I was afraid a soporific might be introduced into the food.'

I complimented him on his prudence.

'Ah!' he groaned, 'I took every precaution…I wanted so much to seize this opportunity…But I didn't get a chance!'

I readily agreed.

'But are you absolutely sure,' I continued, 'that even without a soporific you didn't fall asleep?'

'Oh, Your Honour, not with the danger we were in...!'

I was convinced, and asked no further questions.

Suddenly, M. Louret burst into the room, breathless, an expression of pure terror on his face. Trembling, he handed us a letter, which I read:

"Tonight it will be your turn. There will be as many of us as it takes, and maybe some of us will be left behind, but *you* will be killed! And tomorrow it will be your son's turn. We shall not miss a second time."

We looked at each other in consternation.

'Don't be afraid,' said Dumas. 'I'm going to spend the night here myself. And I guarantee you that, if anything happens, *I* will see it!'

This was clearly meant as a slight to Clement; the flying squad has always been disdainful of the ordinary "flatfoot"….

'Yes,' he continued, 'and it will be better organised. Instead of separating, as was done yesterday, we will all stay together, here in the lounge. And if someone kills you, Monsieur, I'll see the killer, dammit!'

It seemed the obvious thing to do, if not much consolation for the unfortunate Louret, who did not seem particularly reassured.

'If they come in a gang…' he stammered, 'like they said in the letter….'

‘Well then,’ declared the chief superintendent, ‘tonight there’ll be ten officers surrounding the house! Will that be enough?’

‘What about inside?’ stuttered Louret.

‘I already told you I shall be staying,’ replied Dumas, ‘and Inspector Leger will be with me, in whom I have the utmost confidence.’

But Clement, who was still there, insisted on staying as well, wanting, as he said, to atone for his failure of the night before.

‘All right,’ said Dumas, somewhat contemptuously, ‘you can complete the party.’

‘My word,’ I interjected, ‘this promises to be interesting. I’d like to stay as well, if that’s all right.’

I arranged for the notes of my interrogations to be transcribed. As for William, still absent, I replaced his disposition by that of the *gendarmes* who had spoken to him this morning, when he had come to notify them of what had occurred.

At that point, the public prosecutor left, accompanied by my clerk, neither of whom had any desire to stay.

Meanwhile, night was approaching. I made arrangements for the *gendarmerie* to send ten officers around seven o’clock to guard the villa. The shutters were then closed. After which, there was another meticulous search of the premises, with no result.

The inspectors who had carried out the drilling and the other inspections were flummoxed.

‘We’ve been though everything with a fine-tooth comb,’ one of them said to me. ‘And I can assure you that a pin-prick, even one carefully plugged afterwards, would not have escaped our search.’

‘I know my men,’ added Dumas, ‘and if there is the slightest aperture in that room, except the door and window, may I be struck dead!’

‘Needless to say,’ I enquired, ‘you did examine that door and that window?’

Dumas shrugged his shoulders, and I felt ashamed of my question.

‘Yes,’ he said, ‘that was the first thing we did. The bolts were firmly in place during the crime: you can see the damage where the door was pushed in. The window fastening is as effective as it is complicated, which is saying a lot.’

‘Well,’ I commented, ‘at least the fingerprints on the dagger may tell us something.’

‘I doubt it,’ groaned Dumas. ‘That imbecile Pierre Louret pulled it out of the wound! It’s his prints we’re going to find!’

That was very infuriating, I had to admit. And I cursed the presence of such an impulsive individual in the investigation.

The inspectors pressed hard to spend the night along with us.

'Alas, no,' replied their chief. 'There will already be six men in the house, counting his honour the judge and Clement. There will be ten officers outside. I don't want to make a fool of myself and become the laughing-stock of the brigade! I shall only keep Inspector Leger with me.'

So the inspectors left and we closed the door carefully behind them. I noticed that night had fallen. Already the owls were hooting...I had never been stupid enough to be frightened by such noises. But, in the circumstances, there was something decidedly sinister about them....

I confess I had been on the point of following the inspectors. Dumas doubtless read my thoughts, because he looked at me with a knowing smile. Immediately, my self-respect reasserted itself and I decided to stay.

But I had to acknowledge, to my shame, that I was frightened....

CHAPTER V

THE INCREDIBLE NIGHT

'The *gendarmes* will be here in half an hour,' announced Dumas. 'We'll take up our positions for the siege.'

He decided that we would all install ourselves in the lounge, except for Leger and Clement.

The former was told to stay in the first floor corridor the entire time; Clement was assigned the ground floor corridor.

So we settled down in the lounge, except for Pierre Louret, who—as was his custom—remained standing. Beforehand, just as on the previous night, we had distributed lamps in all the rooms, on the stairs, and in the corridors.

'What's really strange,' said Dumas, 'is that we haven't found William.'

'The whole village knows about it,' I observed, 'and a negro is quite noticeable. There aren't that many around here.'

'By the way, what time did you go upstairs last night?' asked Dumas.

'At ten o'clock, we already told you,' said M. Louret.

'Well then, do you know—.' He interrupted himself to address Pierre Louret: 'For heaven's sake can you stop your walking for a moment?'

It was true, the young man was pacing up and down just like a bear in a cage, except that he was also afflicted with an incessant nervous tic. On hearing the order, he sat down, but not for long.

'Do you know,' resumed the chief superintendent, 'what William was doing last night? For, if I've understood things correctly, he wasn't with you.'

'I think,' said M. Louret, 'that he stayed in the kitchen, where we found him at ten o'clock, when we turned in.'

'But didn't you hear him moving about?'

'It wasn't possible, the door of the lounge was shut.'

'Another oversight,' observed Dumas.

'Besides,' added M. Louret, 'I have to say that I trust William as I trust myself. He's more devoted to us than a dog.'

Dumas said nothing: doubtless, in his profession, assurances of loyalty were greeted with scepticism.

There was a long silence, broken only by the irritating hooting of the owls. From time to time, I glanced at my watch. Six o'clock, quarter past six, six twenty-five...I shall long remember that wait…six forty-five…

All of a sudden, at the front of the house, there was a horrible scream, which stopped after a second.

As one, we were all on our feet. Dumas and I rushed towards the shutters, each trying to release one side. I spoke earlier of the complicated fastenings; even though, with two, we took less time than with one person, it nevertheless took several seconds.

Meanwhile, M. Louret was shouting: 'Don't open, for pity's sake, don't open!' As for his son, I caught a glimpse of him slumped in an armchair as if he was about to faint.

At last we were able to part the shutters. The front of the house was quite well lit, although I couldn't, for the moment, discern the nature of the light. And twenty metres away, separating itself from the darkness of the countryside (the moon hadn't yet come out), I could distinguish a figure…

Instantly I pulled out my revolver. Dumas grasped my hand:

'Don't fire, it's Clement.'

Yes, it was Clement. At the same time I realised where the light was coming from; it came both from the lounge where we were standing, and from the room next door (number 2), whose shutters were also open.

Clement turned to face us:

'There is a man here who's been murdered.'

Dumas jumped across the sill and I was about to follow, when a shout from Louret stopped me.

'Don't leave me alone!' he moaned. So I stayed put.

Meanwhile, Dumas shouted to me: 'It's the negro!' With the help of Inspector Clement, he had picked up the body and the two of them placed it close to the window. There, we could see that the unfortunate William had a dagger right in his heart. The form of the handle and the direction of the blow recalled the manner in which Germaine Louret had been assassinated.

'Let's not make the same mistake as last time,' said Dumas. 'Pass me some cotton.'

And, very carefully, he withdrew the weapon and covered the handle, in order to conserve the fingerprints intact.

Suddenly, the sound of voices could be heard outside and shadows could be distinguished in the darkness. Louret had leapt from his chair and was shouting: 'They're here. They're here.'

'Calm down,' I told him. 'It's the *gendarmes*.'

I shook the hand of the corporal, whom I had met several times before, and asked him to provide two men to take the corpse back to the barracks. I say "corpse" because a quick examination had caused us to abandon all hope in that regard. The killer certainly had a remarkably sure hand!

Now Louret, slumped in his armchair, moaned:

'My poor William...They killed him, him as well! They knew he would have defended me!'

'Go and close the shutters of the room next door,' Dumas instructed Clement. 'It was you who opened them in order to get out, wasn't it?'

'Yes, I jumped out through the window when I heard the scream.'

'Shut it, and then let's have a chat.'

Clement obeyed and Dumas and I followed him.

'Explain something to me,' resumed Dumas. 'When his honour and I heard the scream, we rushed to the shutters and opened them together. They're no more complicated than the ones you opened; there being two of us, we must have taken much less time than you. What's more, you, coming from the corridor, had the whole room to cross. Yet, when we finally opened our window, you were already twenty yards away!'

Clement smiled broadly. And he explained that, among the owl hoots, he had distinguished three that were repeated at very close and regular intervals, like a signal. He had listened very carefully; and one minute later, the same effect was repeated.

Thus it was that he had gone into room number 2, and had silently unfastened the shutters, ready to open at once, should the signal be repeated. But, just at that moment, the horrible scream occurred. So Clement had sprung forward; and it seemed to him that he saw a shadow disappearing into the night.

'I congratulate you on your powers of observation,' said the chief superintendent. 'Distinguishing a rhythm in the midst of all that cacophony...'

The fact is that it seemed very strange; I don't know how many night birds could be heard outside.

After Dumas' remark Clement smiled in satisfaction, which had the effect of annoying Dumas greatly.

‘In any case,’ he said tersely, ‘you had no business leaving your post in the corridor. If you had noticed something abnormal, all you had to do was to notify us!’

Clement said nothing; the rebuke was thoroughly justified. He left and I went back with Dumas into the lounge, leaving the door open.

The *gendarmes*, following our instructions, had surrounded the house. Already the moon had appeared over the horizon; in a few minutes, it would be possible to see clearly. So we closed the shutters, much to Louret’s satisfaction.

‘Let’s eat,’ said Dumas. ‘Don’t let the danger spoil your appetite. The gendarmes have brought us an excellent meal. It’s cold, but no matter!’

We sat down to eat. But our appetite had been spoiled quite a bit. M. Louret, in particular, could not eat anything. Was he afraid of being poisoned? Or was it the emotion? This latter theory seemed reasonable. Louret’s fear did indeed appear to grow by the minute. And I noticed the same nervous tics on his face as on his son’s; his hands, also, had started to tremble.

There’s something contagious about terror; I myself was feeling suffocated. And I noticed that Dumas had lost much of his self-assurance; he had stopped talking and was chewing absently on an unlit cigarette in one corner of the room.

Clement was pacing up and down in the corridor; I saw him pass by the open door several times a minute. I was surprised at myself for watching him, as it created more unease than calm…

More to break the silence than because I deemed the moment opportune, I made one more attempt to challenge Louret.

‘If our mission here fails,’ I told him, ‘it will be because you wanted it to!’

He jerked back:

‘Me?!’

‘Yes, you. You obviously know more than you are saying. If you had given us a clearer idea of what was happening…’

‘It doesn’t matter,’ he murmured, ‘…it doesn’t matter where the threats are coming from, if you can’t determine how they’re being carried out!’

‘Come, now,’ I persisted, ‘just a hint…’

Louret squirmed in his armchair, and his distress was painful to see. Then, slowly, he reached into an inside pocket of his jacket and pulled out a slim wallet.

'Look,' he said, as if in a trance, 'it's not much, not much…And yet, it's awful….'

Then, just as slowly, he slid the wallet back into his pocket.

'If I were to die,' he continued, 'you would be able to trace the origins of the affair in here….'

He was unable to finish. Pierre Louret leaped up and uttered a cry so chilling it would have shaken the calmest of men. My heart almost missed a beat, and I saw the colour drain from Dumas' face.

The young man struggled to say a few strangled words:

'Did you hear?…knocks…as if on wood….'

Drawn no doubt by the wild cries, Clement appeared in the open doorway. We all looked at each other, in silent questioning of Pierre Louret's words.

But, suddenly, a cry even more bloodcurdling than the first came from his lips. With a trembling finger, he pointed to the corridor behind Clement. Then he yelled:

'They went past…there…there…in the corridor.'

At that moment, a thought struck me: in the short moment that we were all looking at each other, nobody but Pierre Louret had been watching the corridor. What a monumental blunder we had committed…If, by chance, the young man had also been looking the other way, we would not now have any idea what was happening…And Clement, in the open doorway, had actually been blocking our view…

That thought flashed through my mind, but I didn't have time to dwell on it, for Dumas had reached the corridor with a single stride; he gave a shrill whistle, intended for Inspector Leger, stationed on the floor above; a moment later Leger was at the foot of the stairs.

Needless to say, we had followed behind Dumas, and now we all found ourselves in the corridor.

'No need to panic!' said the head of the *Sûreté*. 'Which way did they go?'

Pierre Louret pointed his thumb towards the kitchen.

'How many?' asked Dumas.

'Quite a few…' stammered the young man.

It seemed to me that, in his panic, the young man had exaggerated; nevertheless, there must obviously have been several.

'Leger and Clement,' ordered Dumas, 'block the corridor!'

So saying, he placed them side by side facing the kitchen, backs to the staircase and the front door, between the lounge door and the door of room number 2.

Naturally, these precautions took only a few seconds.

'And now,' said Dumas to me, 'let's check all the rooms.'

We heard Louret wheezing; he started to whine:

'What about me?'

'Stay with the two inspectors,' Dumas replied sharply. 'You'll be safe there.'

'I'm coming with you,' Pierre Louret announced.

Need I add that every one of us had a revolver in hand?

And we went into room number 2. It was, like all the others, illuminated by an oil lamp. Dumas entered first, I followed, and Pierre Louret, who was last, remained in the open doorway.

'He's so frightened, he's going to shoot us,' I thought. But, in fact, nothing of the sort happened.

At first glance, nothing seemed to be out of place. The room, occupied by Germaine Louret for a long time, contained a few pieces of furniture; we looked around and opened the wardrobe; it probably took us a few seconds.

There was nothing that appeared unusual.

'Now the other room,' said Dumas.

Pierre Louret, who was in the doorway, went first. As we followed him out, we looked to the right, at the inspectors. They had not moved; their eyes were glued to the doorway as we left the room; by a small shake of the head, they confirmed they had seen nothing.

Between them, and very slightly behind, I saw M. Louret; never shall I forget the expression of sheer terror on the face of that man.

Pierre Louret, still ahead of us, had opened the door to room number 3. And straight away he fired a shot and jumped backwards, shouting:

'There they are…there they are! They're getting out!'

With one bound, Dumas and I were in the room.

No armchair, no wardrobe: one glance was enough to tell us there was nobody there at all. Our inspection could not have lasted more than *half-a-second*, at most. At the same instant, violent blows reverberated in the corridor, as if someone was knocking at the front door.

Dumas left the room, shouting at Pierre Louret, who was now facing the inspectors, with his back to the kitchen:

'You're mad! There's nobody….'

The words stuck in his throat. He had just looked, as had I, the length of the corridor. The two inspectors were there all right, frozen, eyes fixed on our door; but M. Louret senior was no longer there!

His son, facing the same direction as we were, pointed to the front door and the stairwell. His mouth was moving, but no sound came out.

'Say something!' shouted Dumas.

And the sound came out in the form of a scream:

'The stairs…they went up the stairs….'

'The first floor!' shouted Dumas.

And so we rushed forward along the corridor.

'Don't leave me here!' screamed Pierre Louret. 'There are more of them!'

So saying, he grabbed my jacket from behind. Undoubtedly he was paralyzed by fright, because I was obliged literally to tow him whilst I was running. I even wondered, at one point, if he would tear the jacket off my back!

Nevertheless, I succeeded in keeping up with Dumas. Side by side, we climbed the stairs, with me still pulling the young man, whose panting breath and muffled shouts I could hear behind me.

At the top of the stairs we found the two inspectors, who had preceded us without ever being out of our sight. All five of us stared at the trapdoor to the attic; the locks and bolts were in their proper place.

'Search the bedrooms!' ordered Dumas.

And he, together with Pierre Louret and myself, stayed at the head of the stairs. The search of the bedrooms, which were practically empty, yielded nothing.

'Back downstairs,' said the head of the *Sûreté* immediately. But, as we reached the downstairs corridor, we were suddenly frozen to the spot.

In the same place where we had last seen him lay Louret, his body stretched out across the corridor….

I felt as though I was going mad. None of us made a sound. Squeezed together in a tight group, we remained motionless….

Eventually Dumas stepped forward and we followed him. The body had a wound at the back of the head. Next to it lay the weapon.

It was a cosh, the latest model. It consists of a hollow sleeve, inside which is fixed a leather strip connected to a lead ball. When not in use, it doesn't take up much space because the ball is inside the shaft; but a sudden forceful movement of the arm will cause the ball to fly out and hit the victim with tremendous force.

We were all standing over the corpse, which was lying face down. A severe head wound was clearly visible because the body had fallen on its stomach.

'He was hit from behind,' murmured Dumas. And he leant over to press his ear to the body.

'Dead,' he announced simply, getting up. 'The blow was violent and well placed.'

We remained motionless, eyes fixed on the corpse, which we were surrounding, as if hypnotised. A crime such as this, in a brilliantly illuminated house…'We didn't see anything or hear anything,' murmured Leger.

'The wallet!' exclaimed Dumas suddenly. He bent over the body once again, and probed each of the inside pockets…'The wallet has disappeared,' he announced after a moment.

I looked for it myself. Nothing…And yet, in my mind's eye, I could clearly see Louret, after showing us the wallet, putting it back in the inside pocket and fastening it there!

There lay the key to the mystery, he told us…We would never learn anything now….

We went back to the lounge in total silence. It was exactly how we had left it. The lamp was on, and the chairs were exactly as we had left them. Pierre Louret had followed us in; he was no longer in an overexcited state; he walked with a blank stare, like a robot, then slumped down in an armchair.

'Now, it's my turn,' he announced simply.

I tried to reassure him.

'No,' he said gently. 'You can see as well as I that there is nothing to be done…These are not men…these are ghosts…ghosts….'

'Don't ask him any questions; you're wasting your time!' Dumas told me brutally. I realised the young man was rambling and I stopped.

There was a thunderous knocking at the front door.

'Ah! The *gendarmes*,' said Dumas. 'I had forgotten about them. Go and explain to them. And let them search everything, that'll keep them amused.'

I recognised the corporal's voice and opened the door. He explained to me that, standing outside, the only noise they had heard was a revolver shot (Pierre Louret's). His men had banged on the doors (the sounds we had heard just before Louret disappeared), but nobody had seen anything. I looked out at the terrace. The moon was already full, and the light was very strong.

'Nothing has moved outside,' repeated the corporal. 'Do you want us to come into the house?'

'If you want...You won't find anything.'

He took a man with him and, for a while, I heard them opening doors and moving furniture...Eventually they came back down.

'Nothing,' said the corporal. 'And everything is perfectly sealed from the inside!'

All of a sudden, I was seized by the fear that I had felt earlier. I thought of Pierre Louret's words: "These are ghosts...ghosts..." Pull yourself together! I told myself; I had never believed in ghosts, and I wasn't about to start today! 'Tomorrow, we'll discover the secret!' I said in a loud voice, as I addressed myself to the corporal.

I gave him my instructions. In the morning, at first light, he was to dispatch one officer to alert the public prosecutor and the medical examiner. The surveillance on the house was not to be relaxed for one moment, for Pierre Louret's life was still under threat. A second *gendarme* was to locate the architect of the villa, the builder, and all the workers involved in its construction.

'I want them here in the morning,' I added. 'I want to question them. Also, find me a twenty-man crew of navvies! I swear to you that I'm going to find the secret passage, even if I have to tear the house apart!'

'Obviously,' said the corporal, 'there must be a passage.'

'We should have looked for it yesterday,' I continued, 'it was crazy to have searched just the one room.'

As the corporal was just about to leave, I called him back to insist that he only send navvies known to him. We had to make sure that we didn't allow the enemy to infiltrate while trying to defend against him.

I also asked him to alert the flying squad as quickly as possible.

'I want ten inspectors to direct the work!'

'Understood,' replied the corporal.

I realised that I was in danger of going too far, and went back into the lounge.

'Two truly extraordinary nights...' I observed to Dumas.

'Never two without three,' he growled.

CHAPTER VI

A BIZARRE INVESTIGATION

The head of the *Sûreté* and the two inspectors, seated in a circle in the lounge, seemed to have given up all pretence at surveillance; and such hopeless abandonment on the part of three such forceful men was itself frightening and discouraging. I sat down with them, feeling utterly drained myself. I had little hope for the measures I had ordered for the following day…We would never know….

If only M. Allou, the real examining magistrate were here! He was bound to have worked it out…What an unfortunate stroke of fate that he had left the very day of the first murder!

In fact, we had almost forgotten about the vagrant…So many things had happened since…So many dreadful things….

My thoughts went back to the last crime. Maybe, at this very moment, the killer was lying in wait for us…Maybe one of us was about to fall victim to those mysterious blows… Too bad, I was too drained, too discouraged; anyway, it might shake things up. Nothing we had tried had worked.

The sound of Pierre Louret's voice brought me suddenly out of my meandering. The young man was muttering:

'Let them kill me right now…I'd prefer it…this waiting…it's unbearable!'

Despite myself, I couldn't help thinking it would be for the best; but I kept that monstrous thought to myself.

I tried to engage the others in conversation, to no avail. All I could get out of them was meaningless grunts… Eventually, a thin ray of light pierced the shutters.

'Daylight!' I exclaimed. Relieved expressions could be seen on all their faces.

'Let's get out of here,' said the chief superintendent. 'We're suffocating in here!'

We went out on to the terrace, where the *gendarmes* were walking up and down to keep themselves warm, for the night had been very cold and the sun was not yet up; I sensed a certain cynicism in the looks they gave me…Dumas frowned and drew me to one side.

'We have to arrest Clement!' he said in a low voice. I was startled.

'Clement! Why?'

'I've been thinking. It has to be him. Look. The night before last he insisted on coming here, and last night he insisted on staying. The night Germaine Louret was killed, he was on guard in the corridor; he is the only one who could have let someone into the room. Yesterday, he was next to Louret at the moment he disappeared. And I've always suspected him of the murder of William; we found him standing over the body.'

'You're crazy!' I replied. 'Even supposing he had wanted to let someone into her room, would Germaine Louret have agreed? What's more, everyone rushed into the corridor when the shots were heard; and from there everyone heard the body fall. Where did the murderer go? Who locked the door on the inside? Don't forget death was instantaneous!

'As for Louret, he was attacked from behind. You can't have forgotten he was in the corridor slightly behind the two inspectors. Your colleague Leger would have had to be involved...And remember. We didn't spend any time in Louret's room; how could he have killed his victim, taken his wallet and got rid of the body?

'And finally, do you think that if Clement had killed William, he would have just stood there by the body?'

'You're right,' conceded Dumas. 'I must be going mad....'

'In fact,' I said, 'I haven't questioned Pierre Louret in enough detail about what he saw last night; perhaps he's got a grip of himself by now.'

We went back into the lounge. In response to my questions, the young man just looked at me as if in a daze.

'Ghosts...' he murmured, 'ghosts....'

'Come now,' I told him, 'you have to be more specific! Who was in the corridor while we were still in the lounge?'

'I don't know...There were a lot of them...Long coats...All those shocks afterwards...I don't remember.'

I knew it was a common phenomenon. An emotional shock could wipe out the memory of everything that happened before.

'You don't know anything about the disappearance of your father either?' I continued.

'My back was towards the front door. A slight noise made me turn round. I saw a shadow disappear up the stairs. That's when I cried out and we all rushed forward...But when I turned back to look, my father had already disappeared.'

I realised I wasn't going to get any more from the young man. It would be better not to insist, for if that stimulated his imagination, he could in all good faith send us on a wild-goose chase.

Dumas had come back into the lounge and was standing in the doorway behind Pierre Louret. Suddenly he stepped forward, looked him sternly in the eye, and said tersely:

'I see that your recollections are remarkably vague.'

He took me by the arm and led me into the corridor.

'Do you want to know what I think?' he said in a low voice. 'Pierre Louret knows much more than he's letting on. But he's afraid to speak. He's hoping his silence will save him, and the mysterious enemy will be grateful. Maybe the father is dead because he told us about the wallet...The son fears the same fate if he talks too much!'

'Yes, that does seem likely...Remember how insistent he was with his sister that she turn the light off at the first sign of attack...He seems to want to protect the identity of the murderer... A bad mistake in my opinion; the killer will show no gratitude but will profit from the continued mystery to strike with impunity!'

'If only the wallet hadn't disappeared,' added Dumas.

'My God!' I exclaimed suddenly. 'There's a desk in Louret's room.'

We hurried there and broke the lock. The desk contained numerous papers which we examined rapidly. None of them seemed to be of the slightest interest. But there could be secret drawers, or documents that were apparently innocent but might yield more on close examination. We were going to need several days to examine everything thoroughly.

'I'll seal the place,' I said, and started to melt the wax. When I had placed the seal on each side of the door, Dumas gave a sudden ironic laugh.

'Do you honestly think,' he said, 'that the thugs we're dealing with are going to respect your pretty ribbons and your dollops of wax?'

I realised how ridiculous it looked....

'Let's go,' continued Dumas. 'I can't stay in this house a moment longer.'

Outside, we walked in silence for a while. Then Dumas called his colleague Leger over.

'Think back,' he said to him. 'Did you really see nothing and hear nothing? Are you absolutely sure?'

His colleague confirmed that was indeed the case, and added:

'The one thing that struck me you know already; while you were looking at the last room, Pierre Louret was standing in front of the door; then, at a particular moment, he suddenly turned in our direction and we all saw his terrified expression. He seemed to see something dreadful....'

With that, Leger left.

'We're not going about this the right way,' Dumas went on. 'Because we have no idea *how* these crimes were committed, we should concentrate on *who* could have committed them...

'We could start by supposing vengeance for some event in the past; in which case maybe Clement is the key....'

'Yes,' I agreed. 'It could equally be Gaston Richaud, Pierre Louret's first cousin, who was completely disinherited by his recently deceased uncle. A particularly lucrative vengeance, because then he would inherit....'

'Obviously,' continued the chief superintendent. 'And in fact it could be Louret senior, so as to inherit from his children; or Louret junior, to inherit the entire fortune...For that matter, who inherits from Germaine Louret?'

'Without a will,' I replied, 'one quarter goes to the father and three quarters to the brother who, as of tonight, inherits everything.'

'Let's see,' said Dumas...One quarter to the father...the uncle left about thirty million...With all the rights, Louret senior's heir collects three million...It would certainly have been worth the effort....'

'You're rethinking Louret senior's guilt?'

'Not necessarily. He could have killed his daughter....'

'But,' I objected, 'it would seem, given that he died shortly thereafter....'

'Maybe his son realised he had committed the first murder; and believing that he would be next, he struck first....'

I thought for a moment. None of that explained in any way the mysterious circumstances of the murders...

'We could go on forever constructing hypothetical cases,' I said. 'Perhaps there were several murderers, each unaware of the others' existence, and who happened by sheer coincidence to act at the same time....'

'Well, that's also possible....'

'And then again,' I continued, 'maybe two or more of them acted together. Unless we suddenly stumble on a secret passage, which I firmly believe is there and which will set us off on a completely new trail....'

But Dumas had stopped listening.

'A conspiracy,' he murmured to himself...Then suddenly, seizing me by the arm:

'Of course, it's obvious. We're stupid not to have seen it before. In the first place, there was a conspiracy between four of them: Louret father and son, William, and Clement. They fabricated a story about the death of Germaine Louret. They were all in it together; they killed her and everything that happened afterwards was a cover-up....'

'But what about the third bullet that hasn't been found? None of them was hit?'

'They fired it through Pierre Louret's open window, to complicate matters.'

'And William's murder?'

'An accomplice who had to be eliminated.'

'What about M. Louret's murder?'

'Likewise.'

'It's not possible.'

'Why not?'

'It doesn't make any sense. If there was another accomplice to eliminate after William, father and son would have got together to get rid of Clement—a stranger, and therefore less reliable....'

'Yes, but the son wasn't going to inherit from his father!'

'Quite. Not only that, it's also physically impossible. Yesterday evening, at the time of Louret's death, Clement never left your colleague Leger; and Pierre Louret was with us!'

'You're right.'

'I think we're barking up the wrong tree. If there was a conspiracy regarding the death of the girl, the *gendarme* on guard on the ground floor would have had to have been part of it. Just remember, he was the one who helped break the door down. And he hasn't been rubbed out, as far as I know...And that would have to be a heck of a conspiracy....'

'All right. But couldn't Gendarme Roustan simply have been mistaken about what happened? Couldn't he have broken down a door that was already open?'

'No, don't you remember he was on the side where the locks were and he actually saw them break: the upper lock first, which then allowed a glimpse of the lower lock before it broke...'

'You're right, of course,' said Dumas. 'As you say, we've been barking up the wrong tree...It's not a good idea to try to reason after a sleepless night.'

'We'll end up suspecting each other,' I said, adding: 'I'm more inclined to think there's a secret passage. And I'll tell you why, at least as far as last night's murder is concerned….

'The passage must go from the lounge to Louret's room. The first thing the attackers had to do was to get us to leave the lounge. That's why they first went along the corridor, where Louret junior saw them. If, by some chance, nobody had seen them, they would have made some kind of noise to attract our attention.'

'But that would still mean that Clement couldn't be in the corridor. Or else, as I said before, he's an accomplice….'

'Perhaps so… but not necessarily. The attackers could have waited until he turned towards the lounge to speak to us. And to cause him to turn, they could have made that slight noise that Pierre Louret heard. Then they went into the father's room, which they left via the secret passage, to reach the lounge which by then was empty. They quietly knocked old Louret out and dragged him into the lounge, where they stayed hidden while we went up to the first floor. They took the wallet and left the way they came….'

The head of the *Sûreté* nodded in agreement.

'Yes,' he said, 'it's a possibility…But they would still have had to guess whereabouts Louret was in the corridor….'

'Oh! That wouldn't have been difficult. Given the state he was in, knowing that he was a prime target, he wouldn't have been out visiting the other rooms with us. Nor would have he been left alone….'

'Yes, but the inspectors could have stayed by the lounge door, or even behind it…'

'No, they had just left the lounge so they knew it was empty. It was a safe bet that they would get as close to us as possible, which meant next to the door of room number 2.'

'You're right,' acknowledged Dumas. 'But do you really think that several men could have come out of the lounge to attack Louret from behind, without being seen?'

'Certainly. Everyone had their eyes fixed on the door of room number 3, where they expected to see the attackers coming out. Anyway, we'll soon find out from the soundings whether there are any secret passages.'

'Yes, I'm beginning to believe your theory,' murmured Dumas. 'In any case, it's the only plausible one…'

A car drove up. I saw the public prosecutor and my clerk get out, followed by a large old gentleman with a white beard, who was introduced to me as M. Rivier, architect.

'It was I that supervised the construction of this house twenty-five years ago,' he announced. 'I can absolutely assure you that there are no secret passages, underground or otherwise.'

'Did you watch the construction work closely?'

'Sir, I never let three days go by without a visit to all my building sites.'

The prosecutor informed me that M. Rivier was born in Aix and had always lived there, and assured me that throughout the forty years of his professional life his reputation had never been other than impeccable.

Then he handed me two telegrams which had been delivered to my office that very morning. The first came from the Paris forensic anthropometric laboratory. It was to inform me that the vagrant's fingerprints corresponded to those of a man given a life sentence of hard labour for murder, five years ago. He escaped under mysterious circumstances as he was being transported to jail. His name was Gustave Bonnet and not Baptiste Florent as shown on the military identification papers found on his body.

The second telegram was from Lyon, informing me that the bank account of Gaston Richaud, Pierre Louret's cousin, showed a clean record; the only item of note was that he had been living with a young person by the name of Louise Blanchi for several years.

The business of the vagrant was getting decidedly more complicated...But I'd resolved to stop thinking about it!

I took advantage of my clerk being there to get a number of statements transcribed. I had only just finished when about twenty workmen arrived, picks on shoulders, preceded by a rotund gentleman in his fifties, who favoured us with a beaming smile.

'I'm André,' he announced. 'André from Puyricard, contractor. It was me that built this house. Ah! I was young then...I'd just taken over the business from my poor father...He died, you know. Died of typhoid fever....'

I cut him short and asked him simply to confirm there had been no monkey business with the villa. But he started off again:

'A passage? An underground passage? Come over here, William! You too, Gaston! And Marius as well!'

Three of the workmen came over.

'Go ahead, ask them. They worked with me...And you can probably find others, if you want to look for them.'

My last hope vanished...It occurred to me, however, that even if there had been no trickery during the construction of the villa, the work could have been done afterwards without anyone in the village being any the wiser. This house was so isolated!

By now, ten inspectors from the flying squad had arrived, so I instructed them to supervise the workmen who were there to dig up the site. They set to with gusto.

Shortly thereafter, the prosecutor, my clerk and the architect left for Aix.

I placed two men on the road outside to keep inquisitive eyes away. The *gendarmes* that had just arrived replaced their colleagues stationed around the house.

And the waiting, the nerve-wracking waiting, started all over again. Nobody was speaking any more, and the only sound to be heard was from the pickaxes. Slowly but surely, tiles were being lifted, walls were being tapped, and a ditch was being dug all around the house...

Nothing, still nothing....

But, at nearly four o'clock, I suddenly saw two familiar figures appear on the road. One, short and stooped, was Bonnet, my clerk. The other, garbed in a wide, flapping, overcoat with a soft felt hat perched nonchalantly on the side of his head was...I hesitated, afraid it might just be wishful thinking...but it was indeed M. Allou, the official examining magistrate!

So he had returned from vacation! What a relief...I hastened towards them.

'Well, my young colleague,' said M. Allou, 'an interesting debut!... A sensational yet simple case....'

'Simple!' I exclaimed.

'Yes, very simple. Don't you think so?'

I thought he was joking, and started to laugh. As we continued to walk towards the house, I asked if he had been brought up to speed.

'Yes, the prosecutor gave me the main points and our excellent M. Bonnet, who misses nothing and forgets nothing, filled in all the detail. I'd already learned quite a bit from the newspapers, and reading this morning's special editions made me decide to come back. You've become quite a star, my dear fellow!'

I assured him I could readily do without it.

'There's one point that no one's been able to clear up for me,' continued M. Allou, stopping to light his pipe. 'The staircase is made of wood, isn't it?'

'Why, yes,' I exclaimed…'But why is that significant? And how did you guess?'

'I thought it was likely. But,' he added looking at the house, 'I was told there was a pigeon house…That's very important; but I don't see it.'

'It's there,' I replied. 'The pigeons nest in the garret. But,' I asserted with some pride, 'I examined it as carefully as the rest of the house.'

'That was completely pointless,' retorted my colleague with equanimity, 'unless by any chance you suspect a pigeon?'

I didn't deign to reply.

'And,' M. Allou went on, 'another important question. Is there a dog or a cat in the house?'

'No,' I replied tersely, starting to feel that the teasing had gone on long enough.

'Are you sure?'

'Absolutely sure.'

We had arrived in front of the villa.

'And what are all these good men doing?' continued M. Allou, indicating the *gendarmes*.

'They are supervising…'

'Haven't you realised yet how useless they are?'

I stammered something incoherent.

'That seems very cruel. Haven't you thought, confirmed bachelor though you are, about the wives and children anxiously waiting for them at home?'

He called the corporal over and told him his men could leave, including the two on the road outside; as it was nearly nightfall, there were unlikely to be sensation seekers about.

I was stunned.

M. Allou went into the house; the workmen were making a deafening noise; the ten inspectors were running to and fro.

'Are you giving a reception?' my colleague asked.

I blushed to the roots of my hair….

'Please order them to stop,' he continued, 'I can't stand the noise. And we shouldn't increase the costs of justice.'

'It was so that we could see what was underground,' I stammered.

'You are too inquisitive, my young friend. Why do you care what's underground? Unless you are thinking of buying the house. You may go home,' he said, addressing the inspectors and the workmen.

'You're sending everyone away?' I gulped in embarrassment.

'Everyone except perhaps the dear chief superintendent,' he continued, noticing Dumas. 'How are you?' They shook hands. 'I'll keep inspectors Leger and Clement as well, since the press is talking about them. Rest assured, my dear young colleague, that there will be enough of us, including the excellent M. Bonnet, to play some interesting parlour games tonight.'

I couldn't think of anything to say.

'What would you like to see?' asked Dumas.

'The most comfortable armchair in the house,' replied M. Allou. 'But, before we start, gentlemen, I want to make one thing very clear. If I ask one of you a question, only the person I ask should respond, even though someone else may feel themselves better placed to answer or to interrupt.'

We went into the lounge. Pierre Louret was there, the workmen having finished some time ago. His agitation of the previous night had gone, to be replaced with a despondency which was, if anything, more disquieting.

He stood up as we entered and M. Allou introduced himself.

'First of all,' he continued, 'please accept my condolences for the tragic deaths in your family.'

'Ah!' replied Pierre Louret, 'The sorrow is almost more than I can bear. But I know that I shall not suffer much longer…Tonight it's my turn.…'

The examining magistrate nodded his head sadly.

'I cannot lie to you' he said. 'I, too, fear that you are in great danger.'

'Your Honour,' cried the young man 'I don't want to stay here any more…This house will be the death of all of us…It's haunted…haunted.…'

'Perhaps…' murmured M. Allou.

'So, you won't have any objection if I leave…disappear altogether…so that nobody can find me.…'

'Quite frankly, I think that's in your best interest, and probably your last hope…But will the people that are chasing you let you go?…I only ask that you wait until I've finished my investigation here; I may have certain questions to ask of you.'

'Will it take long?'

'No, not very long. Maybe a few hours; I see a lot of ground has already been covered. But I can promise you that before eight o'clock I will take you back to Aix with me. That will be better for you....'

At that, Pierre Louret seemed somewhat reassured. But, knowing the fury and power of his mysterious adversaries, I wondered if Pierre Louret wasn't deluding himself.

'Because you're here,' continued M. Allou, 'I'm going to ask you some questions right away; questions that may perhaps have been overlooked. Forgive me if you have already answered them.

'First of all, what is your opinion of Gaston Richaud, speaking quite frankly and without reservation?'

'My Goodness, Your Honour, I don't quite know what to say...I only saw him for a few days each year; and even though we were closely related, that doesn't mean that we were on particularly intimate terms....'

'Do you think he was capable of murder?'

'Really...I don't know....'

'Fine. Second question. How did your uncle Maurat die a month ago?'

'We were walking in the fields together, the two of us. Suddenly he collapsed in my arms. I called out for help, but there was nobody to hear. Eventually, a peasant happened to pass by. He helped me carry the body back to his place. But by that time my poor uncle was no longer alive.'

'Fine. Third question. The evening of your sister's murder, did you hear the noise that Clement noticed, like someone knocking on wood?'

'No, even though I had my window open, which you doubtless know?'

'Actually, no; I thought that only the shutter was open. The cold must have prevented you....'

'I was wrapped in a long dressing-gown which reached down to my toes.'

'I understand. So despite the window being open, you heard nothing?'

'Nothing.'

'At least that's what you say...' murmured Dumas. But M. Allou shot him such a sharp look that he said nothing more.

'Your father,' continued my colleague, 'was, I've been told, a man in robust health. Do you think he was capable of defending himself effectively against attack, even unarmed?'

'Certainly; he boxed and I sparred with him; I can assure you he was very good at it.'

'Thank you, that's all,' concluded my colleague.

While he was talking, he had been twiddling a pencil around in his fingers. Just at that moment, he hit the table with it, breaking the lead.

'How could I be so clumsy!' he exclaimed. 'M. Louret, can you lend me your penknife? I've forgotten my own.'

Dumas made a move towards his own pocket. But he had been so affected by M. Allou's look a few moments earlier that he froze in mid-gesture. Pierre Louret offered my colleague a small flat knife with two blades, opening the larger one.

M. Allou started to sharpen his pencil.

'This doesn't cut properly,' he said. 'Maybe the other blade is better?'

'No,' insisted Louret. 'On the contrary, it's worse.'

'In that case,' concluded M. Allou, smiling, 'with all due respect, your knife is worthless. My dear colleague, do you by any chance have one?'

I realised then that M. Allou was toying with us or seeing just how far we would go in respecting his instructions. These proceedings were starting to irritate me!

Pierre Louret asked him:

'Before I go, can I sort through my father's papers to see which ones I need to take?'

'Of course, my dear monsieur, that's quite normal.'

'But his desk is sealed....'

'Yes, I thought...,' I murmured.

'There's no need for it,' continued my colleague. 'Break the seals. Only the upstairs rooms are out of bounds. Call the inspectors.'

Leger and Clement, who had been waiting in the kitchen, came into the room.

'Go to the corridor upstairs,' ordered M. Allou. 'Nobody is allowed to go into any of the rooms under any pretext, and that includes you. Do not come down until you hear your chief's whistle. Before you go up, close all the shutters, starting with this room. And turn off all unnecessary lights. You're going to bankrupt the Republic!'

'I will see you when you're ready, my good sir,' he continued, turning to Pierre Louret. 'Take all the time you need. As you can see, I have an enormous file to study.'

The young man left the room.

I was anxious to know how this unlikely investigation would continue. The joy I had felt at the beginning had given way to a vague unease…It seemed to me that we were chasing trivia and ceding the villa to the enemy. All surveillance had practically disappeared…

M. Allou went to the clerk's briefcase and withdrew a printed form which he wrote on for several minutes in one corner of the room. Then he folded it in two and put it in his pocket.

He had used the corner of a chest of drawers while he was writing. He opened the top drawer and closed it again immediately.

'I've finished,' he announced.

'So now what do we do?' I asked.

M. Allou stretched out in an armchair.

'We wait here,' he replied.

'You will want to examine the file, no doubt?'

'You must be joking! That huge pile! Haven't you heard about my legendary laziness yet?'

And he lit his pipe.

'So,' I said. 'Why stay here?'

'We're waiting….'

'Waiting for what?'

'The last crime….'

CHAPTER VII

THE LAST CRIME

I recoiled at these words and Dumas nearly jumped out of his skin.

'There's going to be another crime?' I almost shouted.

'I believe so,' replied M. Allou, calmly.

'But that's dreadful...Poor Louret, we've left him by himself...'

My colleague regarded us gravely.

'I do indeed fear that he is lost,' he said. 'Now it's his turn.'

'We have to do something!' shouted Dumas.

'And what exactly would you do?'

The question left us speechless...Obviously, everything we had tried up to now had not met with any success....

'I note,' continued M. Allou, 'that your experience has left you wiser. Believe me, I am utterly convinced that nothing can save Pierre Louret. In any case, I can't do anything for him.'

A profound dread overcame me and the most extraordinary suspicions began to form in my brain...I could see Inspector Dumas was thinking the same. Only the clerk, slumped in his armchair, remained inscrutable; nothing M. Allou did could surprise him.

'All the same,' exclaimed Dumas, 'we can't just sit here and do nothing, if only because it's our professional duty!'

'Professional duty?' retorted my colleague. 'What is our job? Is it to prevent crime or to find the perpetrators? We are here, as you well know, to apprehend the guilty parties, not to try in vain to save a man who, I repeat, is already lost.'

It was harsh, but perhaps true. What a weight to have on one's conscience! In the final analysis, there was nothing to be done except follow the judge's instructions. Nevertheless, I asked him:

'You presumably found some facts that we overlooked?'

'No,' he replied. 'With regard to the facts of the case, I know nothing more than you. Tell me, dear colleague,' he started again after a short pause, 'what did you decide in the case of the theft of coffee from the display window? Did you question the sales person?'

I replied rather sharply that I had more important things to worry about than that minor affair, and other things to occupy my time!

‘It’s true,’ conceded M. Allou, ‘you’ve gone to a great deal of trouble…However, I did tell you the proper method: listen to the statements, read the police reports, and the truth will out all by itself…It’s automatic…When one is young, one always works too hard!’

I didn’t reply…The silence became prolonged….

‘Since you have discovered so much,’ I said somewhat aggressively, ‘maybe you could tell us the exact time when the next crime will occur?’

‘I don’t know yet…But I’ll let you know ahead of time, I promise.’

I felt a cold hand on my heart. Dumas was showing clear signs of nervousness. Bonnet, the clerk, seemed to rouse himself and was stirring in his armchair...This third night, as Dumas had forewarned, seemed ominously likely to be even more terrifying than the first two….

The silence was broken by M. Allou’s calm voice:

‘Are there any interesting balls this season, my young colleague? At your age, you must love to dance?’

I gave an evasive response, then took a couple of paces in the room and looked at my watch: it was nearly seven o’clock.

‘Do we have much longer to wait?’ I asked, almost at the end of my tether.

The judge seemed to be deep in thought; he made a sign that he did not want to be disturbed. Then he looked up:

‘Two or three minutes, four at most,’ he announced calmly.

I thought that my heart would stop; I asked breathlessly:

‘We still don’t move?’

‘Not yet; let me remind you we are only involved with crimes that have been committed.’

In fact, M. Allou had not even put his pipe down. Dumas and I waited anxiously…I was grasping my watch and mechanically looking at the hands as they moved….

One minute…Two minutes…Three minutes….

And at that moment three shots rang out in the house!

At the same time, a voice that I recognised, that of Pierre Louret, screamed: ‘Help! Help!’

Dumas and I rushed to the door.

‘There’s no hurry, it’s over,’ declared M. Allou calmly, putting down his pipe.

We didn’t dare run; and the clerk, even more shaken than we were, couldn’t have run even if he had wanted.

'You're the ones in danger now, gentlemen,' said M. Allou calmly. 'Call the inspectors.'

Dumas blew a whistle; Leger and Clement appeared at the foot of the stairs. All five of us, following the examining magistrate, approached room number 3, M. Louret's old room, where his son was supposed to be working.

'Open up!' shouted M. Allou.

We heard the huge interior bolts being drawn and Pierre Louret appeared. I noticed immediately that his jacket was slashed from top to bottom.

'I've been wounded!' he moaned.

Our eyes swept the room and took in the horror…On the floor lay the body of a man. At the same instant, I noticed with dread that, once again, the shutters were closed!

We went closer: the head was covered in blood. Leger leant over and listened for a heartbeat:

'He's dead,' he said, standing up.

'I can well believe it,' agreed M. Allou. 'Seeing that he has two bullets in his head…There's blood on the jacket…Unbutton it…Yes, another bullet in the heart!'

We didn't recognise the dead man.

'It's my cousin,' stammered Louret. 'It's Gaston Richaud….'

'Ah!' I said, 'That's what I thought!'

For I had immediately forgotten all my earlier suspicions.

'What happened?' demanded Dumas.

The young man started to faint. We brought an armchair close and he slumped down into it. We opened his jacket and were immediately reassured. There was only a long gash on his body, starting just below the heart. Undoubtedly, the weapon must have slipped to one side. We noticed the dagger—a small triangular weapon—close to the body, similar to the ones we had seen before.

'What happened?' asked Chief Superintendent Dumas again.

'It's fantastic,' said the young man. 'I was working at the desk; I had barricaded the shutters and the door…Needless to say, I had examined the room beforehand and it was empty. All of a sudden, I heard a noise behind me…you know…like knocks on wood. I turned round swiftly: Gaston Richaud was there before me, with a dagger in his hand. In one incredibly swift movement, he cut me in the chest. Thanks to my boxing ability, I was able to parry the blow with my left hand. At the same time, I used my right hand to retrieve my revolver from my jacket, and fired a first round through the material. My adversary staggered back. I freed my weapon and finished him off with two shots to the head.'

'It's just as mystifying as ever,' murmured Leger. 'How did he get in?'

'And now,' I declared, 'it's all over. We know the culprit, but we still don't know his secret!'

Imperturbably, M. Allou sat down and produced a new pipe from one of his pockets, which he proceeded to tamp down and light up. His calmness was becoming exasperating.

'This is your revolver, is it not?' he said to the young man, indicating a weapon that had been thrown on the table. He picked it up, examined it for a moment, then placed it next to his person.

'Are you feeling better, M. Louret?' asked Dumas.

'Yes, thank you, much better,' replied the other, smiling. 'I believe I am safe now....'

'Don't fool yourself,' M. Allou replied tersely. 'You've never been in more danger than you are now, as you're about to find out!'

We were all seized by a collective dread, but nobody dared move a muscle.

CHAPTER VIII

THE SECRET

'Now that you're feeling better,' resumed M. Allou, 'you can answer, if you will, two questions that I neglected to ask previously. First, why did you throw the bodies of pigeons with their throats cut, around the countryside?'

'Pigeons with their…It wasn't me!'

'You deny it? Yet someone saw you.'

'Oh, well…Yes it's true. I didn't dare admit it for fear of making a fool of myself…It's a superstitious practice….'

'Why did you go out of sight of the house to get rid of the bodies? Williams, the negro, would certainly have understood. Answer the question!'

The young man hesitated:

'I don't know,' he murmured.

'Fine. Second question. Why is the pocket of your dressing-gown stained with pigeon's blood? I recognised it under the microscope!'

An agonising silence followed these words. Then Pierre Louret mumbled:

'I don't know…I don't know…There's a lot of strange things happening here.'

M. Allou stood up, and his face took on an expression which frightened me. His steely gaze transfixed Pierre Louret. Without warning, he went up to Louret and roughly seized the twin-bladed knife we had seen shortly before from his jacket pocket.

'I shall simply make a small scratch with the small blade,' said my colleague. 'We shall see whether it really does not cut, as you claim!'

The young man recoiled, frighteningly pale, and cried out in an anguished voice:

'No, you have no right…I forbid you…let go of that knife....'

We were about to intervene but M. Allou put the pen-knife in his pocket and, with his penetrating gaze still on Pierre Louret, announced:

'I see that I was told the truth. Regarding your sister's murder, Clement saw everything and is fully aware of what happened. He didn't dare say anything at the time, because he was afraid of William, who had a dog-like devotion to you. Later, he was still afraid to speak because, as you know as well as I, he could equally well have committed the crime himself, using the same method; and the belated revelation would have made him a suspect. I only got the truth out of him a short while ago.

'Regarding your father, you overlooked the mirror in the hall, where everything was reflected; Dumas, as he turned the stairs, saw everything. But, before proceeding further, he wanted to wait for William's murderer to return.

'Finally, those are your fingerprints that will be found on the dagger.'

So saying, he nodded towards the weapon, which lay beside the corpse on the floor.

A terrible look crossed Pierre Louret's face; there was fear but, above all, anger and hatred.

'Ah!' he cried out. 'You've had luck on your side! Well, so be it, I've lost, but I'm a good sport, you'll see. What's the point in denying anything? I'm better than all of you! It was brilliantly conceived, admit it. And without your blind luck, you'd still be nowhere!'

At that, M. Allou drew from his pocket the paper he had prepared in the lounge.

'Do you have the guts to sign this?' he asked.

'Why not? As I said, I'm a good sport; I lost, so I pay!'

He signed, then held out his hands to inspector Leger, who handcuffed him.

'What did he sign?' I asked.

I had actually recognised what he had been given: a questionnaire for first appearance in court.

M. Allou sat down and calmly proceeded to light his pipe, which had gone out during the last dramatic minutes.

'Clerk, please read it out,' he said simply.

M. Bonnet stood up and read in a dull voice:

'You are charged with the voluntary homicide on 15 November in Avignon of your uncle M. Maurat; with the voluntary homicide on 27 November in Puyricard of a vagrant, name unknown at this time; with the voluntary homicide on 1 December of your sister Germaine Louret; with the voluntary homicide on 2 December of your father Paul Louret; with the voluntary homicide on 3 December of your cousin Gaston Richaud. All these crimes with premeditation.'

The clerk turned the page and continued:

'I admit the crimes of which I stand accused. *Signed*: Pierre Louret.'

There was a collective gasp of shock and outrage. But M. Allou had resumed his habitual calm. He said with a smile:

'Wasn't I right to tell you Pierre Louret was lost? Do you still believe he can still keep his head?'

'All these deaths…' I murmured…

'Plus which,' added Dumas, 'you've forgotten one: William, the domestic help.'

'That wasn't him,' said M. Allou.

But, on hearing Dumas, Pierre Louret looked startled.

'What,' he shouted, 'so you didn't know….'

The examining magistrate started to laugh.

'I lied to you, Louret. Neither Clement nor Dumas saw anything at all, nor did anyone see you tossing dead pigeons away. It became apparent to me what must have gone on as I went through the whole business step by step. However, you must realise that I needed your confession…The truth is the most flattering outcome for both of us: you plotted very well and I detected very well. Good show!'

'I saw so little,' observed Clement, 'that even now that I know the culprit, I still don't understand anything!'

'Neither do I,' I added. 'I was a firm believer in an outside force; some sort of vengeance.'

'That's readily excusable,' said M. Allou. 'Louret senior believed the same thing. I suspect that man of having a shady past during his time in America, which made him fearful of terrible reprisals. Crime is in that family's blood…Louret was mistaken, the killer acted purely for money.'

'The wallet,' mused Dumas. 'We could have learnt some interesting things from the wallet. But maybe you know what happened to it?'

'It is, in fact,' replied the judge, 'in the top drawer of the chest in the lounge where I noticed it a short while ago. Monsieur Bonnet, would you please be good enough to fetch it?'

The clerk left the room and returned a moment later, holding the wallet that Louret had showed us the evening of his death.

'Monsieur Allou,' I said, 'I beseech you, explain to us what happened.'

'Willingly,' he replied, 'But I gave M. Louret my word earlier on, that I would take him back to Aix with me this evening. I want to keep my promise. Would you be good enough, Clement, to go down to the village and instruct the police to send us two cars, for I sent mine away when I arrived; I wanted to make sure, for obvious reasons, that the house did not appear to be guarded. And, once we have this gentleman in a safe place, you will give me the pleasure of dining with me, for I have taken the liberty of ordering dinner in advance. I will give you a thorough and accurate account of the events...in which you participated.'

Nobody noticed the irony of that last sentence…Soon afterwards, two cars arrived, provided by the inhabitants of the village. Seven of us got in.

And not long afterwards, we were, except for Pierre Louret detained in prison, gathered at M. Allou's residence, where we partook of an excellent meal in front of a blazing fire.

CHAPTER IX

EXPLANATIONS

'Don't make us wait any longer!' I implored.

'Ah!' replied my colleague. 'I'm savouring my revenge…Admit it: just a short while ago, you and Dumas were doubting my motives....'

I blushed in acknowledgement. But after all, the way he conducted the investigation, the steps he took, the nerve-racking all-night session, and all the terrible shocks we endured over the two days….

'I forgive you,' said M. Allou.

And he started his explanation.

'I must admit I didn't work it all out in strict chronological order, nor did I perceive all the details for each case at the time it happened. In other words, if I had been there with you during those tragic events, I wouldn't have fared any better than you at preventing them.'

We found some consolation in these words and managed a few smiles. M. Allou went on:

'The first murder I solved was that of Louret.

'Five people, in addition to the victim, were in the house: my young colleague, Chief Superintendent Dumas, Inspectors Leger and Clement, and finally Pierre Louret.

'Leger and Clement did not leave their posts: at the instant that Louret disappeared they were side by side. Their reputation is too honourable for me to suspect them….'

The two inspectors expressed their thanks with broad smiles.

'…but I did anyway,' continued M. Allou, 'because it was my duty to look at all the possibilities. However, they could only have done it if they had worked together, which made it even more unlikely.

'But above all, during the second that you were in Louret's room, they wouldn't have had time to knock him out and get rid of the body; the more so because his son had stayed in the corridor and had turned round even before you came out. To cap it all, how would Leger and Clement have managed to put the body back in the corridor afterwards?

'I couldn't suspect my colleague or Dumas either, because they were at the other end of the corridor and from then on they were in Pierre Louret's line of vision.

'That left only two possibilities: Pierre Louret or an outsider.

'In this regard, I had the young man's account of events.

'Now, not only was that account suspect, it was also evidence against him.

'If he had in fact seen the men in his father's room before you went in, they would not have been able to escape except via a secret passage. They would have had to act at blinding speed: first impossibility.

'What's more, if the passage did exist, it would have been known to Louret senior, because it was he who had had the villa built. And it couldn't have been built later without his knowledge: the house was always occupied and the owner only went away for short trips to Marseilles. Hell's bells! You can't dig a hole in a wall or a floor so easily! That's the stuff of newspaper serials!

'And if this passage had been known to Louret, even supposing that he had his own reasons for concealing it from us, he would not have stood at the lounge door with his back turned to the room, which he knew to be a possible direction of attack!'

That now seemed self-evident to me.

'Besides,' continued M. Allou, 'the murder of Germaine Louret had occurred beforehand, and a microscopic examination of her room had revealed no secret openings. Therefore, the truth lay elsewhere.

'That left only Pierre Louret, who had clearly lied. I therefore started to look at him more closely.

'What leapt out at me was his facility for creating an atmosphere of terror, which seemed to have played an important role in the events as they unfolded. You must surely remember his bloodcurdling shriek the night before, at the instant that shots rang out in his sister's room. And remember his extreme nervousness on the evening before his father's murder. In addition, the murder of William—which he had not foreseen—contributed beautifully to the overall atmosphere.

'Remember also the terms of the anonymous letter Louret received. It was awful. It said: maybe some of us may be left behind, but *you* will be killed. A threat made that much more frightening because the previous night's prediction had come true, and in the most mysterious fashion.

'Words cannot express the depth of Louret's fear that night, particularly since he did not have a clear conscience. The publication of his photo in the newspaper, the words attributed to the vagrant, the letters he received: all that convinced him that his whereabouts were known and his score was about to be settled.

'His behaviour was therefore quite predictable and consistent with anyone else in that situation.

'All of a sudden his son emitted the dreadful shriek you described, which was the final straw and which plunged the father into a state of abject terror, which was certainly genuine. The shriek had the added effect of bringing Inspector Clement to the door.

'The evocation of knocks as if on wood enhanced the effect and caused you to look at each other questioningly. The moment was ripe, because there was no one watching the corridor, to pretend to see people there.

'Pierre Louret was careful to use the plural noun: they're here! And somewhat later, he would tell you there were quite a few of them. Thus the threats in the letter had come to pass...Louret senior believed he was finished; he surely knew the determination of those he feared.

'His reaction was quite predictable. He didn't join you during your search of the rooms, where he could be shot at point blank range. He wouldn't stay alone in the lounge either. So his place had to be between the two inspectors, who would take up positions as close as possible to those searching the rooms, with their backs to the lounge which they knew to be empty.

'If you hadn't placed the two inspectors there, my dear Dumas, Pierre Louret would have acted differently; but it was highly improbable that you would leave the corridor empty while you were visiting the rooms!'

'I wouldn't have made such a mistake,' agreed Dumas.

'That was anticipated. So, you visited room number 2: nothing. And then, if you recall, Pierre Louret, who had not until then appeared particularly courageous, went into room number 3 ahead of you. And, no sooner had he opened the door, he shouted: "They're here, they're getting out!"

'Remember what was written in the letter: "maybe some of us will be left behind"...Those words were not selected by chance any more than those that were shouted: "They're getting out." If in fact they were getting out, Louret, smack in the middle of the corridor, was a sitting duck for anyone willing to sacrifice their life to get him. They would have the time to fire before they were taken down. Right at that moment, as if any further complication were needed, the police could be heard banging on the front door!

'Louret had the predictable reaction. In order to give you time to kill or arrest the attackers, whom he believed had been discovered in the room at the end, he ducked into the lounge to hide.

'The inspectors, their eyes glued to the bedroom door, waiting tensely for the appearance of the men that had supposedly been seen, did not notice Louret's manoeuvre. Also, remember that Louret was slightly behind them at the time; his reaction was quite predictable and born of fear.

'Once in the lounge, Louret turns out the light by way of further concealment. Then he starts to plot his revenge; he takes out his wallet, which contains what he assumes is the reason for the attack. Even if he is killed, the murderers will be killed in turn by your men; they won't be able to search the house, so the wallet will be found at a later date and will reveal who was behind the crime. So he puts the papers in the nearest place he can find, in the only drawer in the room.'

'How did you work that out?' enquired Dumas.

'It was,' replied M. Allou, 'the only explanation possible for the disappearance of the wallet. So I was not surprised at all to find it in the drawer, which was the first place I looked.

'During the couple of seconds that Louret took to hide in the lounge, you all came out of the room; and, following Pierre Louret's directions, you rushed towards the stairs.

'That young man, who had turned round and spotted his father ducking into the lounge, knew perfectly well what he would do next; nothing in the world could make him stay downstairs alone, especially after his son had shouted: "Don't leave me here! There are more of them!"

'Now, from that moment on, *you were no longer looking at Pierre Louret!*'

'But,' I interrupted, 'he never let go of my jacket, and I could hear his heavy breathing behind me!'

'I repeat,' insisted my colleague, 'you were no longer looking at him. He only needed one hand to hold on to your jacket; the other hand was free. As he heard you going past, Louret senior rushed to the lounge door so that he could join you, exactly as his son had anticipated.

'But as you went by, you didn't see him. Why not? First of all, because you were running, and all your attention was on the staircase ahead. Secondly, because the lounge was in darkness. It was because you didn't notice anything that I deduced that the light had in all likelihood been turned off a few seconds earlier.

'You pass by the door. That's the moment for Louret senior, who has no intention of staying downstairs alone, to hurry out to join you. At that very instant his son, who's immediately behind you, is level with the open lounge door.

'Without breaking stride, he uses his free hand to launch the lead ball from the cosh; as you know, it can be deployed in a fraction of a second. It's easy for him to strike his father in the back of the head, for he's much taller and in good shape from his boxing training.'

'Now I understand,' I observed, 'why you led him to talk about sport earlier on.'

'You'll understand even better in a moment, because that revelation was doubly significant. Thanks to his agility, the fatal blow was delivered with such rapidity that the victim didn't even see it coming and had no time to cry out.

'Bonnet told me that, at one instant, you had the impression that Pierre Louret was going to tear your jacket off your back. That was due to the slight slowing down necessitated by the crime.

'The blow was extremely violent, due to both the young man's power and the speed he was going. As for the father, who had been rushing to join you, he took two or three more steps forward before collapsing in the middle of the corridor, where you found him. His son, as he turned towards the staircase, threw the truncheon and sleeve behind him.'

'But,' observed Dumas, 'we didn't hear any noise of a falling body.'

'That's why I deduced that it was a wooden staircase. Five men running up the stairs must have made a considerable din. And remember how thick the carpet was in the corridor.'

'It was still a considerable risk,' I said. 'What if Dumas or I had chanced to look back just as the crime was being committed?'

'Oh, that's no trouble! Pierre Louret would simply have said: "I saw a shadow coming out of the lounge; I was afraid and I lashed out." And in the nervous state he pretended to be in, that would have seemed quite understandable!'

'True,' I conceded…'But was the lounge indeed in darkness? I remember quite clearly that the lights were on when we went back down.'

'I was told,' replied M. Allou, 'that when you went back downstairs you were only interested in the body; that you all stood around it as if hypnotised. Meanwhile the killer walked calmly into the room and lit the lamp again. The corridor was already well lit, so the added light would not have been noticed.

'Besides, even if you had noticed, what the young man did would have appeared quite natural. But seeing that you hadn't noticed, he kept quiet about it, not wishing to draw your attention to the fact that the lounge had been dark when you went past; that might have made you pause to think.'

'Even so,' I insisted, 'it was still a very risky crime. If Louret senior had not been killed on the spot, he would have denounced his son as soon as he regained consciousness. And the story of the mysterious shadow would not have held water, because it would have been inexcusable for Pierre Louret not to have told us he had just hit someone.'

'I thought about that,' said M. Allou. 'And I concluded that the murderer must have had some sure way of achieving his ends, in the unlikely event that he didn't succeed first time. I say unlikely event, because the weapon was formidable and was wielded very effectively.

'What sure way? That set me thinking about Maurat, the uncle. If the young man had committed the heinous crime of parricide, he certainly wouldn't hesitate to kill his uncle.

'Because the murder of the father could only be explained by greed about the inheritance. And Maurat was the original source of the inheritance. He died of a heart attack. Maybe it was from natural causes…but maybe it was poison…Internal or external? In the food or by injection?

'This hypothesis of poison made me think of Gaston Richaud who was, you will recall, a chemist. And, in fact, there must have been someone else implicated in this whole business. William's murder could not have been committed by Louret junior, because he was in the lounge with you at the time. And, as I will explain later, if Richaud was involved in the death of the uncle, it is highly likely that he was also involved in the death of the servant.

'If Maurat was poisoned by injection, then there was in fact no risk involved in the death of Louret senior. Pierre Louret was certain to render him unconscious at the very least. And then, if that were the case, it would have been easy for him to administer the injection that had worked so well with Maurat at some point while he was holding his father in his arms. It would have been assumed that the death was a natural consequence of the blow to the head.

'But, I repeat, that was only a precaution for the worst case, to make sure that all possibilities were covered and to assure that, whatever happened, the murderer would not run any risk. From what I've heard he didn't need to take it.

'I was certain, however, that he had planned for the worst; he was too astute not to have done so. It was to reassure myself on this point that I questioned him about the death of his uncle. Do you remember: it happened out in open country, with no witnesses? Therefore, it must have been by injection. And the murderer must certainly have kept the weapon in order to use it on his father.

'What kind of weapon?

'Pierre Louret was too careful to have kept a syringe or a lancet, or even a needle. In the event he was searched, that would immediately have attracted attention. As natural as it was for him to have daggers, revolvers, and coshes, such an object would have appeared suspicious.

'I concluded that the poison could only be on an object which appeared harmless but which could be sharpened. That object could well be a knife.

'That's why I broke the lead in my pencil and asked him for a knife. I knew that he dare not refuse me, because we might have seen it in his hands and could in any case have searched him and found it; a lie would have aroused suspicion. What's more, he wasn't taking much of a risk by handing it over. He just had to make sure I wouldn't use the poisoned blade.'

'Why?' I asked.

'Because if I were clumsy enough to cut myself and drop dead on the spot, that would have been enough to expose him. Now, the long blade which he opened for me, cut perfectly well. Nevertheless, when I wanted to use the shorter blade, he told me it was "even worse." His haste to discourage me told me all I needed to know.'

'I've understood everything as you've explained it,' I said. 'But I must admit that I'm still in the dark about Germaine Louret's murder!'

'I'm getting to that now,' replied M. Allou. 'I had found a plausible theory for the death of the father. It had led me to suspect that Maurat had been murdered.

'I readily concluded that, if there was a monstrous individual evil enough to commit such crimes, he wouldn't hesitate to kill his own sister. And, in point of fact, the father's death would have been pointless unless he had already inherited from the daughter. So her death must have been by the same hand.

'I tried to imagine how Pierre Louret could have done it.

'Do you remember how nervous Germaine Louret was? Her father told you that she fainted very easily. That's what her brother was counting on, although—as you will see—the loss of consciousness was not vital to his success.

'Do I need to remind you how adept this young man is at setting the stage? He starts by placing a letter in the mailbox, which reads: "You and yours are condemned to die." First shock for the young woman. Then, the same evening, he simulates an attempted break-in through the shutters of her room, with a double objective: to reinforce the advice to extinguish the lights when under attack; and to stretch the young woman's nerves to breaking-point.

'He comes back into the house as soon as his sister starts to scream. And the reason his father finds him at the foot of the stairs is not, as you thought, because poor Louret lacked the courage to go outside immediately; it was because he had just come in through the front door and had not had time to go any farther. Otherwise, his father would have seen him pretending to come down the stairs.

'How did I reach that conclusion? Because the servant, who lived on the upper floor, just like Pierre Louret, nevertheless did not make an appearance until some time after him.'

'However,' I pointed out, 'Louret junior needed time to get back inside the house; how did he get there before his father?'

'You're not making allowances for reflexes. Pierre Louret rushed to the front door at the *first* scream from his sister. Neither his father nor the servant woke up right away; they did not realise immediately what was happening. That short delay gave Pierre Louret ample time to get back into the house and close the door; at the time, nobody thought to check the locks and bolts, because the danger appeared to be coming from elsewhere.

'The next day, another menacing letter, even more threatening: "We failed last night. We will try again tonight." Clement, you told me about the ensuing evening gathering and the daughter's anguish. The letters, the attempted break-in, the feeling of panic…the likelihood of fainting became greater and greater. You can imagine the state the poor girl was in when she went to bed.

'Her brother had found a good pretext—surveillance of the house—for leaving his window open. Once Gendarme Vaneau had turned the corner of the villa, Pierre Louret took a cane, leant out of his window, and rattled his sister's shutters. That's the noise that Clement heard—

"knocks on wood"— and which the culprit repeated the next day to increase his father's anguish.

'What happened next was entirely predictable.

'The young woman cries out in terror, picks up her revolver and, following the advice she has repeatedly been given, extinguishes the lamp; then she fires in the direction of the window.'

'She might as well not have fired,' I commented.

'True, but it would have made no difference, as you will see. Even though the sound of the shots had shaken Germaine Louret, she had—against all odds—not yet fainted; or at least the murderer could not be sure that she hadn't.

'That's when, while leaving his room, he emits the frightening shriek you described. That's the last straw; you hear the noise of her falling, the young woman has fainted.

'The culprit, I deduced, was wearing a long dressing-gown; it was to establish that fact that, when I questioned him earlier, I tested him about how cold it must have felt with the window open. You will soon learn what purpose it served.

'The door is broken down and you see the body stretched out. Away from the blinding glare from the corridor, you can't see very clearly…Clement gathers the young woman in his arms.

'Just at that moment, the brother approaches and leans over, his dressing-gown trailing on the floor. Under the gown he's hiding a container full of blood.'

'The pigeons!' I exclaimed.

'Yes, pigeon's blood. He lets fall the container, which you don't see because the dressing-gown is touching the floor. With his foot, he pushes it against the body which Clement is holding, crushes it, and then presses it against the clothing. Being now flat, it's hardly visible.

'Then he points out the blood to Clement, who believes the crime has already been committed and it's all over; he drops the body and goes to light the lamp. Meanwhile Pierre Louret leans over his sister, who's still alive. His weapon is hidden in his wide sleeve, and while he clutches his sister to his breast…he stabs her!'

We could not suppress a murmur of horror. A crime like that, in cold blood…For several moments, no one spoke.

Clement spoke first:

'But why did he make me come into the house?'

'It was the father's idea. And the son backed him up: the more witnesses the better. Your presence, and that of the police officers, allayed the suspicions which might otherwise have fallen on the inhabitants of the house.'

'So,' asked Dumas, 'if the fainting had not occurred, would the plan have failed?'

'No, a fellow like that leaves nothing to chance. When you went into the young woman's room, if she had been standing up, a direct blow to the heart would have knocked her out; and it would have been easy for someone with training to have carried it out it in all the darkness and confusion. A young woman would not have offered any resistance. After which, the plan would have continued as planned. You can now grasp why my probing about sports was doubly significant.'

'Sorry to ask such a silly question,' I said, 'but why did you immediately assume it was pigeon's blood and not chicken's or rabbit's?'

'It's quite simple,' replied M. Allou, with a laugh. 'A chicken makes a noise when its throat is cut, and William would have heard it. A rabbit is silent, but its blood is black and viscous and could not pass for a human's. Besides, I knew that there were pigeons in the house, and when I arrived I noticed there were no hen houses or rabbit hutches.'

'But,' I insisted, 'how were you so sure that he had thrown the pigeon's bodies in the open countryside? Your question certainly made an impression.'

'What else could he have done with them? Leaving them in the house, which was about to be searched, would have been too risky; their discovery would have been food for thought, so to speak. Giving them to William to cook? I think he might have been quite surprised!'

'He could have quite simply have got William to kill them to have for lunch,' I suggested.

'Then there wouldn't have been any blood. A chef wouldn't bleed a pigeon!

'And also, you confirmed there were no cats or dogs in the house who could have eaten the bloodless pigeons' corpses... Remember the importance I attached to that question; but you thought I was joking!'

I offered silent acknowledgment. M. Allou continued:

'I was saying then, that the blood was put in a container, which I assumed the murderer would dispose of as quickly as possible; but it must initially have been in the pocket of his dressing-gown. That's why I asked him about the bloodstain.'

'What about the third bullet,' asked Dumas suddenly, 'the one we couldn't find?'

'It wasn't the third: it was the first. Pierre Louret, sometime earlier that day, had removed it from its cartridge and replaced it with some kind of packing.'

'Why?'

'To lead us to believe that the culprit had been hit by it before he disappeared! You all fell for it, by the way. You all believed there was someone in the room when the shots were fired!'

'But why did William disappear the following day?' asked Leger.

'Oh, that's easy!' replied M. Allou with a laugh. 'He was a negro, and like all his race, he had a mortal fear of ghosts. And, for him, there could be no other explanation. Admit it, my dear colleague, the same thought had occurred to you!'

Blushing, I had to admit it had. M. Allou continued:

'Poor William was utterly devoted to his employers. But, faced with what he thought were ghosts, he felt defenceless. Even though he no longer dared put his foot in the house, he nevertheless felt it his duty to keep watch in case there was trouble.

'So, at nightfall, the poor devil approached the villa, even though fear had kept him away during the day. That's where he found Gaston Richaud as he was sending his signal. He jumped on Richaud, but ended up getting stabbed. It's all very simple.'

'Not that simple,' I protested. 'What was Gaston Richaud doing there?'

'He had supplied the poison to kill his uncle....'

'How do you know that?'

'It's a reasonable assumption, seeing that he was a chemist; we'll have to see whether the facts bear me out. If I'm right, he provided the poison because he hoped to benefit from the death of his uncle. Which is why his fury knew no bounds when he learned that he had been disinherited.

'I don't know why the will was like that. Perhaps Pierre Louret knew how to get around his uncle? Perhaps Maurat had an old debt to settle in favour of his brother-in-law, as a result of their stay in America?

'Whatever the reason, Richaud decided, in his rage, to demand an explanation from his cousin. But he preferred to arrive without being seen; if Pierre Louret had refused to budge and would not give him his proper share, I believe he was prepared to take the ultimate revenge;

in which case, it would be better not to have been seen by the rest of the family.

'And so he resolved to arrive at night and to gain entry by using a pre-arranged signal, probably dating from the days when he lived in the villa and went out on night-time adventures with his cousin.'

'I noticed the signal,' interrupted Clement, with some pride.

'That's right,' confirmed Dumas, 'And, because I hadn't noticed it myself, I suspected you, I must confess. But why didn't you warn us about it, instead of going out alone?'

Clement blushed and admitted:

'I so wanted to distinguish myself by finding something, to redeem my failure of the night before!'

'I assume,' continued M. Allou, 'that at the time Gaston Richaud was unaware of the murder of Germaine Louret. The newspapers had not yet reported it, because it had happened just as they were going to press. And Richaud, because of his plan for revenge, did not show himself in the village, where somebody might recognize him. No doubt he arrived directly from Marseilles and knew nothing. But I thought he might try to return the next day—in other words, tonight.'

'Why?' I asked.

'Precisely because he found out about the crimes this morning, just as I did, from the newspaper special editions. Pierre Louret was not naïve enough to tell anyone, least of all his cousin whom the will deprived, about the projects he had in mind; and Richaud had no reason to suspect them, for he was merely a simple killer and not a dreadful monster like his cousin.

'So, Richaud was startled by the news of the two murders. All the papers talked about the presumed motive: revenge for something that happened in America; and it seems to me that he must have believed that, because, for the family, that was a strong probability. After all, the children knew something of the troubled past.

'Now, the grandfather that the two cousins had in common had lived, as you know, in America, where Louret senior had known him—and had even got married on his return to France as a result of that contact.

'Who was being threatened? Was it just the Lourets that were targeted, or should we look further back? And, most of all…most of all, where exactly was the danger coming from? This question, you can readily understand, was of the essence to Richaud. And only Pierre Louret could provide the answer; he should have information through his father having confided in him, or papers found after his death; in any case, he was the only hope.

'But he needed to hurry. Because, in Richaud's mind, Pierre Louret was in the same danger; he was going to be killed, like his father and sister; and doubtless that very night. Richaud had to see him as soon as possible.

'But—as you noticed as well as I—Louret was waiting for him; he even isolated himself for that purpose.'

'I made Richaud's task easier by openly calling off the surveillance...Were you wanting him to come?' I interrupted.

M. Allou gave me a quizzical look.

'No,' he replied, 'I can't say that; I can't say it because I knew that if he came he would be killed...and I couldn't *wish for the murder*; I merely contented myself with doing nothing to prevent it. I was within my rights, because it was none of my business.'

'But how did you know he would be killed?'

'Pierre Louret had two reasons for killing him, both equally powerful. First of all, he had absolutely no intention of sharing his inheritance; you don't kill your father and your sister in order to enrich a cousin. Now, Richaud was dangerous because of his poisons, and his revenge was to be feared. After the murder of William, Louret knew that his cousin could be quick to act...and he, too, was fearful of being a recipient of the famous heart-attack, which would have left Richaud as the sole remaining heir.

'Secondly, Louret could divert suspicion once and for all; all he needed to do was to simulate an attack—which, in fact, is what he did. Those were the two motives for which Louret opened the door at Richaud's signal, his revolver at the ready.'

'But,' I objected, 'if Richaud was only looking for information from his cousin, why did he arrive surreptitiously? Why didn't he just ring the doorbell as you or I would have done?'

'First of all, because it was unlikely that he had given up the idea of vengeance. But most of all because, the night before, Clement had almost surprised him at the very moment William was being killed and saw him running away; he didn't know to what degree he had been noticed, and so was fearful of being recognised.'

'But,' observed Dumas, 'suppose, despite your theories, Richaud hadn't come?'

'Oh, it wouldn't have made any difference; I would have arrested Pierre Louret anyway....'

'So, why let him in? '

'Why stop him? We could have brought a serious charge against Louret that way; to simulate an attack, he would have had to shoot himself; and there was a chance of finding his fingerprints on the weapon.

'Don't feel sorry for Richaud. I have thought long and hard about him. If he arrived clandestinely, after having given the same signal as the night before, he would prove himself to be the mysterious visitor that Clement saw last night. He would thus be William's killer; the first reason for not being interested in him. What's more, the very fact of his secret presence the night before seemed to me to prove his involvement in Maurat's murder: he was coming to claim his reward; if not, why would he have taken so many precautions and why would he have killed William?

'I repeat, I didn't have the right to wish for his death. But because it was all supposition and deduction on my part, I had a perfect right to ignore it all and let events take their course. Our first duty was the arrest of the Lourets' murderer.'

'You just spoke about the signal; I presume it was because you had just heard it that you announced that the crime would take place in three or four minutes; how did you know it would happen so fast?'

'Surely you don't think,' smiled M. Allou, 'that Pierre Louret was going to stop and chat with his cousin, at the risk of being heard or—even worse—let him strike first? He had nothing to say to Richaud and it was better for him to act immediately after the shutters were closed.'

'I have one last question for you,' said Clement. 'Why did you send us to guard the upstairs corridor?'

'Why, to prevent Louret, who had just talked about his dressing-gown, trying to remove the traces of blood upstairs, in case he hadn't already thought of it. And in fact, as I told you, he had not taken that precaution, probably because he was worried about being caught in the act, which would have been an unnecessary risk if he was not under suspicion.

'And I told you not to go into the bedrooms or to return downstairs without instructions to do so, because I anticipated that Clement, just as the night before, would notice the signal. If he had looked out of one of the windows, Richaud would have run away. If you had come down to warn us, Louret, hearing the racket you would have made coming down the stairs, would not have opened the door for his cousin. On the contrary, giving the order in front of Louret actually reassured him. Furthermore he didn't know, nor did his cousin, that the signal of the previous night had been detected by Clement, because we had questioned him away from the lounge.'

'And obviously,' I remarked, you didn't want to do anything to prevent the murder of Richaud.'

'Nothing, as I told you. It was my right and I accept full responsibility. Now, all that's left to investigate is the banal story of the vagrant; I assume, my dear colleague, that you've worked that one out?'

'I believe so,' I replied. 'Pierre Louret ran in to him purely by chance on the road. And he fabricated an attack, to give credibility to the notion of reprisals against his father and his family. He even went so far as to place twenty thousand francs in his victim's wallet.'

'Yes,' confirmed M. Allou, 'I made exactly the same assumption. And it wasn't by accident that he faked the revenge attack; he seemed perfectly familiar with his father's troubled past and the papers in the mysterious wallet; in fact, he didn't seem to need to look for them after Louret senior's murder.

'And he was no doubt perfectly happy for us to find the papers, knowing they would send us on a wild goose chase!

'We'll examine everything at our leisure tomorrow. For tonight, it's late and you are all tired, so go home and rest.'

As we were leaving, Leger, at the door, observed:

'He's nevertheless a remarkable killer. To commit all those crimes without a break…'

M. Allou smiled:

'I think I know the reason, but I don't want to say it for fear of offending you…'

'No, please. Go ahead.'

'Well, my friends, just think about it. Pierre Louret couldn't repeat the heart-attack routine without arousing suspicion. So he needed deaths that were more violent; and he took advantage of the fact that he had highly-placed and sympathetic witnesses to divert attention from himself…'

'Yes, the moment was ripe,' I murmured gloomily.

CHAPTER X

COUP DE THÉÂTRE

We left; it was midnight.

The clerk of the court left us immediately, his wife not being accustomed to him coming home so late. Dumas, Clement and I walked together in silence.

'I'm cold,' said Clement, 'and I'm very tired. Let me say goodbye here; I think it's just about to rain and I'd like to get home as soon as possible!'

The sky was indeed covered by cloud.

Clement walked quickly away, and I noticed that Dumas kept his eyes fixed on the figure, which gradually faded into the night.

'I should follow him,' he growled. 'We would certainly find out some interesting things…But no; he is astute enough to notice!'

I was stunned by these words. What! Chief Superintendent Dumas was not entirely convinced of Clement's innocence, even after my colleague's succinct explanations? Really, what a remarkable display of job conditioning!

I told him as much. But he replied:

'I am a better observer than you. Don't take offence: I have had a long career in the police force. Didn't you notice anything when we arrived at M. Allou's house?'

'No,' I replied in bewilderment.

'Didn't you see a man stationed close to the door?'

'Yes, perhaps…I didn't really pay attention.…'

'And did you notice who came into the house last?'

'My goodness, no. I remember that M. Allou went in first to light the stairs. I came in behind him.…'

'Yes,' continued Dumas. 'As for me, I stood back to let Clement come in. But he declined so modestly that I didn't insist. But I watched him out of the corner of my eye, without him noticing…I know how to do that…And I saw him quite clearly make a sign to the man who was waiting!'

I was absolutely astonished by his claim…M. Allou's explanations had seemed so convincing.…

'Do you think my colleague was barking up the wrong tree?' I asked.

Dumas didn't answer my question right away. After a few seconds, he continued:

'I don't believe there was any signal: that owl's hoot repeated...I'm a good observer, as I told you, and I would have noticed just as well as Clement.'

'But this evening M. Allou heard it as well!'

'I can only repeat that this evening neither you, nor I, nor Leger noticed any such thing.'

This time Dumas had gone too far and his professional jealousy had driven him too far. I observed curtly that he was doing nothing short of accusing my colleague of lying, not to mention complicity.

But he protested:

'No, no, I didn't say that. I merely said we don't know everything...By the way, just between the two of us, and off the record...Do you approve of your colleague knowingly allowing Gaston Richaud to be killed?'

Dumas' lack of respect was becoming more than I could handle. I told him brusquely that it was not my place to pass judgment on my colleagues, and even less was it his place. So saying, I turned and walked away from him.

But I soon began to sense that my indignation was not entirely well-founded. There was something niggling me....

I had taken a long time to get to my flat, because M. Allou lived on the outside perimeter, in the area farthest from the city centre and the least populated. I had never really given it much thought; for the first time, I wondered why he had chosen to live so far from the *Palais de Justice*. He had in fact explained it to me once; he hated noise and could not live in a street where more than one person passed by in any given half-hour....

Why had he allowed Gaston Richaud to be killed?

And then there was the extraordinarily penetrating insight! How had he so easily found the solutions to puzzles which had eluded Dumas and me? And with such incisiveness and certainty?

It had started to rain and I'd pulled up the collar of my coat. Nevertheless, I didn't walk very quickly, as I wanted to sort out my thoughts before I got home....

But I reached my front door in the same state of uncertainty, and still very annoyed with myself. Another thought occurred to me: why had M. Allou held on to the famous wallet, which he had found so easily?

Suddenly, I made a decision. My colleague's holiday was not officially over; therefore I was still in charge. I would take advantage of the situation tomorrow, and interrogate Pierre Louret myself...

Despite my fatigue, I woke as early as usual. And at eight o'clock I set out for the *Palais de Justice* in rain which was by then falling very heavily. On the way I stopped at a kiosk to get my usual morning newspaper. But the vendor asked me:

'Why don't you take the *Éclair de Marseilles* as well? It has all the details of the Cypress Villa business!'

I was thunderstruck. How could M. Allou's explanations already be in print? Wasn't he the only person to have found the solutions? Had someone else done so at the same time...or earlier?

Once in my chambers, I read the four-column article. The case had been very accurately reported. On my desk there was a note from the public prosecutor's office expressing astonishment that a newspaper had been informed before the judges of the court.

I gave orders for Pierre Louret to be brought before me at once; there was nothing to prevent this, as he had not asked for a lawyer the previous day. Two *gendarmes* brought him to me at nine o'clock and I started my interrogation.

All trace of nervousness had disappeared and he answered the questions calmly. He confirmed every one of M. Allou's deductions.

No, decidedly, there was nothing more to be learned beyond what we already knew. There was no point in continuing with additional questioning. But I was face to face with the most odious monster imaginable. I could not contain my indignation.

'How can you have committed such a series of crimes?' I exclaimed. 'How can the lust for pleasure reach the point that it can transform a man into a beast?'

Pierre Louret gave me a peculiar look.

'I don't give a damn about your pleasures,' he said mockingly.

I exclaimed again:

'It wasn't for the money? Then I don't understand...was it just for the love of crime?'

'Not that either.'

'Then explain it to me...I don't see it....'

The young man sneered:

'Ah! Your Honour, you may have found out a lot of things, but this is where it ends! Maybe your colleague will be more astute...Talk to him...As for myself, I'm not going to say any more, at least for the time being!'

In vain, I continued to press him. I was beside myself as a result of his insolent tone.

'Why are you so obsessed with psychological motives?' he asked. 'Isn't it enough to know how the crimes were committed? You weren't so inquisitive last night: where does this anxiety come from?'

A man who is certain to be condemned to death can afford to be insolent to a judge. So I sent him away, as if his manner had not affected me (it was the easiest thing to do). The interrogation had lasted more than fifty minutes and it was nearly ten o'clock.

As he reached the door, Louret turned back:

'I will talk perhaps...later...I'll see....'

With that, he left.

I remained perplexed. Was I the butt of a joke? Was the accused preparing a method of defence which was not yet ready, and which he wished to perfect at his leisure?

I didn't have time to dwell on such matters. Suddenly, shouts rang out in the *Palais de Justice* and I ran out of my chambers.

The general air of panic led me to believe that something very serious had occurred. And I quickly learned that Pierre Louret had just escaped!

Straight away I phoned the neighbouring *gendarmeries* with instructions to pass my warning on. All roads in France, all stations, all ports were to be watched. The detailed description of the fugitive, prepared that morning in prison, was communicated simultaneously.

While the public prosecutor's office was initiating its process I launched my own enquiry into the escape. And this is what I found.

The accused, guarded by two *gendarmes*, had descended the stairs without incident and arrived in the main hall, the *Salle des Pas-Perdus*, which opens directly on to the street. About twenty people were there, seemingly unaware of the prisoner; the guards suspected nothing.

But suddenly, as if on a pre-arranged signal, fifteen or so men rushed the guards simultaneously and knocked them down; then, encircling Pierre Louret, they rushed him towards a car which was stationed, engine running, in front of the main door of the *Palais*. The car drove off instantly and the assailants scattered to the four winds.

The whole business had only lasted two or three seconds. Several barristers and solicitors who were there had had neither the time nor, doubtless, the inclination to intervene; but they had had a clear view of the assailants: none of them was known to them.

I was bewildered. This intervention from the outside, on the suspect's behalf, smacked of advanced planning. Obviously M. Allou was not quite as astute as he believed…Unless.…

I decided to brief him immediately on what had happened. Maybe he would draw a conclusion which I had overlooked?

The actions I had set in motion after the escape had taken some time, and it was eleven o'clock before I could start out. I learned, as I was leaving, that the red car which the assailants had used had just been found abandoned about one kilometre from the *Palais*. It had been stolen that very morning from an honourable member of the bar who sat on the Court of Appeal.

CHAPTER XI

THE PLOT THICKENS

I walked as quickly as I could, head down against the buffeting rain. There was not much risk of bumping in to anyone: the slightest sprinkle causes all the natives to vanish indoors, and today it was a veritable deluge.

It was a considerable surprise therefore when, turning the corner on to the boulevard, I saw quite a gathering in front of M. Allou's house. I had a sudden feeling of unease, and started to run.

'What's happening?' I asked the first person I met.

'M. Allou has just been killed!'

For a second, I stood stock still, dumbfounded. Then, getting hold of myself, I went as quickly as I could up the two flights of stairs separating me from my colleague's landing. A difficult climb, because of the densely crowded staircase.

There were two police officers in front of the door. I questioned them sharply:

'When?'

'Less than three minutes ago!' answered one of them.

I entered the vestibule. To my right was an open door to a room which overlooked the boulevard; the body of M. Allou lay doubled up against the window.

I took several steps in that direction and bumped into someone whose arm I instinctively seized. I recognised Clement immediately.

'What are you doing here?' I asked him.

'Nothing…nothing. I was coming…someone fired just a moment ago…I haven't moved from here. The killer is still here…he couldn't have left!'

At this point two more officers arrived. I ordered them to search the flat while I approached the body. I discovered with relief that my colleague was still breathing.

'Quickly, get a doctor!' I shouted.

I was told that someone had already gone to find one.

As far as I could tell (the doctor would confirm my observation), the victim had been shot in the back of the head. The flow of blood had started; evidently, judging by the limited spread, the crime had been committed very recently.

The room where the victim lay was a bedroom. I noticed that the window it was under was open. I also noticed that M. Allou was only wearing a dressing-gown on top of his pyjamas, as if he had been shot just after he woke up.

However the officers had searched the whole flat and there was nobody hiding there! There was only one item out of the ordinary: the desk in the office had been broken open, seemingly with some force, as if by someone in a hurry. I instantly recalled my colleague placing Louret senior's wallet there the night before, as we were leaving the room.

I immediately went to look: it was no longer there.

'Ah! The miserable wretch!' exclaimed Clement. 'No sooner did he escape than he thought of revenge!'

At that moment the doctor arrived. But his arrival had provoked a new and more aggressive attitude amongst the onlookers packed into to the stairwell. In an instant, the two brave officers guarding the door were pushed back and twenty or so people invaded the flat in the doctor's wake.

For several moments there was an intense crush. Then the two officers that had been searching the rooms joined forces with their beleaguered colleagues; and the crowd was pushed back again on to the stairs.

The doctor approached the victim and examined him closely.

'It's difficult to tell with certainty,' he said, 'but maybe a trepanning operation will save him. Before I left my clinic I phoned the hospital; an ambulance should be here at any moment.'

It arrived almost immediately and took my colleague away.

Since there had obviously been a crime, I decided to take charge and start my investigation at once. One of the officers would serve as clerk. I installed myself in M. Allou's office and sent for Clement.

'Could you explain what you are doing here,' I asked, 'and what you have seen?'

'I came to warn M. Allou about Pierre Louret's escape.'

'And who told you to come?'

'Nobody…I thought it was the right thing to do….'

'You certainly have plenty of initiative, Mr. Clement. It's certainly curious—.'

'Your Honour, it didn't square with what the judge told us last night. I was anxious to learn what explanation he would offer.'

‘All right, let’s go on. Tell me everything you saw.’

And Clement explained the extraordinary event as follows:

He had arrived at the house barely five minutes before me. He had rung M. Allou’s doorbell several times but received no answer.

He had been about to leave when he heard someone coming up the stairs. It was my colleague’s housekeeper, whom he had seen the previous night. She was returning from the market, with her basket full. Clement asked her if she expected her employer back soon. She replied, somewhat surprised, that she had seen his mail still in the glass-fronted mailbox, where it had been when she left for the market; hence it was almost certain that M. Allou had not gone out.

While she was speaking, she tried the key in the lock. But the door would not open…Together they had shaken it and realised that the lower part of the door would not budge.

‘He hasn’t gone out,’ said the housekeeper. ‘The door is bolted inside. No doubt he’s still asleep; you didn’t ring long enough.’

Clement retorted that he had indeed been ringing for quite a while, and furthermore it was already eleven o’clock. So they had both banged loudly on the door, but with no response. Then the housekeeper abruptly observed that it was very strange for her employer to have got up to lock the door, which had not been locked at eight o’clock, and then gone back to sleep afterwards…Maybe it was not he who was locked in the flat?

‘Mademoiselle,’ said Clement at that point, ‘go out into the street, where I noticed two officers who are probably still there. Bring them back here at once. I’ll wait on the landing.’

She had hardly reached the corner of the street when Clement thought he heard someone groaning. He didn’t hesitate any further and threw himself against the door to break it down. The bolts were nothing compared to those of Cypress Villa; and the inspector, strong as an ox, broke them open at the first attempt.

Scarcely had he set foot in the flat, than he heard a shot. A second later, he was in the vestibule and saw M. Allou collapsing in the position where I had found him.

Clement had then stood there a moment motionless, expecting to see the murderer who, inevitably, would have to leap past him to get away. But nothing happened.…

Then the two officers had arrived, followed shortly afterwards by all the neighbours. And only a few more minutes later, I had appeared!

I had listened to the inspector’s account without interruption, despite it being highly implausible.

'It must be fate,' I remarked. 'Yesterday, you came upon William's body at the very moment he had been hit. And today, the same thing happens with M. Allou.'

'Yes,' replied Clement, 'it's frightening...and, as you saw for yourself, there was nobody in the flat...It's starting again, just like back there...Pierre Louret's schemes....'

'Excuse me,' I said drily, 'but there was somebody there: you!'

Clement's face twitched.

'You suspect me?' he exclaimed.

'I'm going to continue the investigation. Make sure you're available.'

And I ordered the two officers to keep him under observation. Then I called in the housekeeper.

She was a stout lady in her fifties with a round red face.

Regarding the meeting with Clement, she confirmed his story. Then she added that at eight o'clock that morning, she had opened M. Allou's shutters, as she normally did except when she had specific orders to wake him. He must have been tired, because he continued sleeping.

'But, even so,' she added, 'he's never slept until eleven o'clock before...I don't understand why he didn't let us in. Ah! He was a fine gentleman, the judge; you have to be a villain to kill a man like him! Do you think he'll pull through?'

I promised her he would, on the off chance. Then I got her to confirm that she'd left for the market around nine o'clock. At that time, M. Allou had still not stirred and she had not seen him.

I questioned her about the other tenants in the building. She told me that was easily done. For a long time, the ground floor had been rented by an electrician; he had gone bankrupt and, since he returned to his native village a month ago, the shop had remained closed and empty.

On the first floor lived a "maiden lady"—to use the housekeeper's expression—who had to be seventy years old if she was a day.

As for the floor above us, the third, it comprised attics to the north, a central corridor, and two rooms to the south whose windows—slightly smaller than the others—could be seen from the boulevard. The two rooms were intended for the use of the servants of the first and second floor tenants. But the first-floor tenant, Mlle. Escoiffier, only used a cleaning lady; hence only the second of the two rooms was occupied.

'Why don't you live here in the flat?' I enquired.

'Oh, sir! With a bachelor...Don't even think such a thing...And in any case, there's no room.'

I should have realised that. M. Allou had only two rooms and a kitchen which overlooked a street to the east. The room serving as his office had two windows, opening to the north on a garden; his bedroom overlooked the boulevard to the south. When you entered the flat through the small vestibule, the kitchen was straight ahead, the bedroom to the right, and the office to the left.

I sketched out a floor plan, which is shown below.

I asked the housekeeper again:

'You say you went to open M. Allou's shutters at eight o'clock, so presumably he had not locked the door? Was that normal?'

'He only locked it when he didn't want me to come in....'

'Meaning....'

'Meaning...when he was not sleeping alone...You mustn't reproach him, Your Honour; I'm told that happens with lots of high class people...But last night there was nobody there!'

I felt it was my duty, no matter how much I might be embarrassed, to ask her a number of questions about my colleague's private life. I must admit that, from a strictly moral standpoint, it was not entirely unblemished....

'My goodness, sir,' the housekeeper confessed, 'he did have young people here....'

'Always the same?' I asked.

'Yes, always the same, but it changed...Do you understand?'

'No, not exactly...How could the same change?'

'I mean...it was the same for one month, maybe two...And then, without anyone telling me why, it would change.'

'What sort of women were they?'

'Oh, Your Honour, they were not what you might call high class young ladies, to be sure....'

'I assume not. Did they have a profession?'

'Yes, they were working class, secretaries mostly; the last one, a really pretty thing, was an apprentice milliner. But, for more than two weeks, there hasn't been anyone.'

'I understand. Tell me, did he send them away, or did they leave of their own accord?'

The housekeeper shot me an indignant look:

'Your Honour...how could you think that they would have left the judge voluntarily? Is that conceivable?'

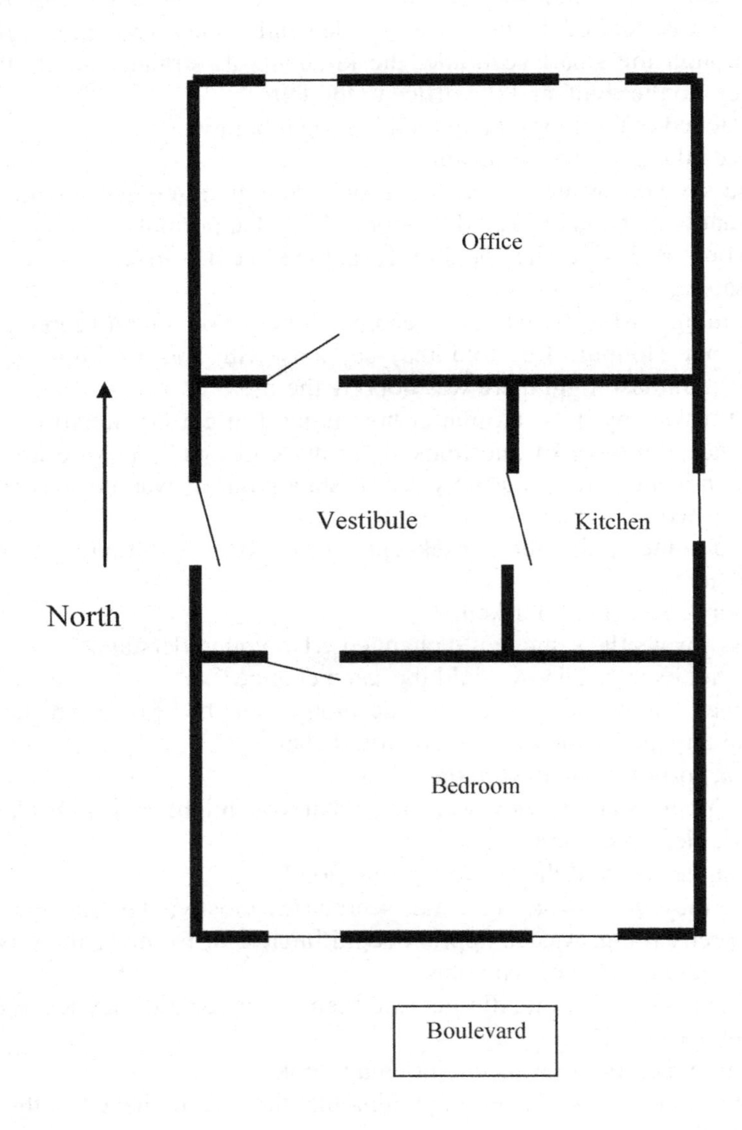
Office
Vestibule
Kitchen
North
Bedroom
Boulevard

I sensed that I had just touched on one of those delicate and unspoken sentiments dear to the hearts of maiden ladies…Clearly there was a risk of taking a wrong turn in my investigation. Nevertheless, I pressed on:

'Under the circumstances, do you think there is any possibility of revenge, from jealousy…'

The housekeeper daydreamed for a few more moments….

'No,' she said, after a while, 'I don't see anyone who…There were never any violent scenes. A few tears…a little gift…and it was over. Do you understand?'

'Perfectly.'

The possibility of a *crime passionnel* seemed to recede. What was more to the point: how could the young woman have got out?

I sent for Mlle. Escoiffier, the first-floor tenant. To be honest, I didn't think she would know anything about the affair; but, on the contrary, her testimony turned out to be of crucial importance.

I saw a very old lady enter the office, her face as wrinkled as a prune; but her clear blue eyes were as young and alert as those of a sixteen year old. Her voice was soft and somewhat affected; her sentences constructed with extreme care. Mlle. Escoiffier informed me she had been a teacher for forty years.

'Your colleague, sir,' she began, 'was a very fine man. He never failed to greet me when he saw me on the stairs and exchange a few words, always very respectfully....'

'I don't doubt it, mademoiselle. But do you know anything about the crime?'

'Do I know anything? Why, my dear sir, I know everything. Everything!'

'Everything? Then tell me quickly, who is the culprit?'

'Ah! That, sir, is the only thing I don't know. I didn't see anything, but I did hear everything.'

'Tell me quickly!'

'It was like this, my dear sir. It must have been eleven o'clock or thereabouts, to judge by the alarm-clock in my kitchen, which is only slightly slow. But I must first tell you that the chimney in my bedroom—which faces south, immediately above that of my unfortunate neighbour—that my chimney gives out smoke just after I light the fire….'

'Yes, yes. Please skip the details!'

'But it's not a detail, as you'll see. So just now—it must have been about eleven o'clock—I lit the fire. And, as usual, I opened the window to draw the smoke out. At that moment, I saw M. Allou's housekeeper in the street; she'd just left the building and was running. She had scarcely turned the corner of the street when I heard a loud noise in the house. I learned later that it was M. Allou's door, which Clement had broken open.

'At the same time—yes, at the same time, Your Honour, or so soon afterwards that it's not worth mentioning—the window above mine was flung open and I heard your colleague's voice. He shouted: "Help!"

'But he didn't have time to shout it twice. For, straight away, there was the revolver shot and I heard the sound of the body collapsing on the floor in front of the window. You can't imagine how quickly it all happened...A few seconds at the most....'

'Your testimony is remarkably precise,' I said to the old lady. 'Let me see if I've understood properly, because it's very important. The sequence of events was as follows: someone breaks the door open, M. Allou opens the window and shouts for help, then there's a revolver shot? You're sure that's the sequence?'

'Absolutely sure...But, as I say, quickly, very quickly.'

'Then what did you do?'

'I leant out of my window and shouted for help. The boulevard was deserted. But just then I saw two officers emerge from the street next door and run into the house.'

'So nobody could have got away after the shot?'

'Nobody, Your Honour, I can assert that unequivocally. Either I would have seen the murderer—who wouldn't have had time to run downstairs, by the way; or he would have run into the two officers. I came up the stairs behind them and I saw the man, the one you just questioned, Clement, standing in the vestibule. He didn't move, and the officers, who were guarding the door, dared not move either. They were waiting for the murderer to come out...In the blink of an eye there were people everywhere...It's amazing how quickly a shot will attract people. The houses next door emptied in an instant. It's true that I shouted loudly...You arrived almost at once....'

I thanked Mlle. Escoiffier for her valuable evidence. Then, in turn, I questioned the two officers, who confirmed all the foregoing statements.

They had been, as I said, in a side street where they could see the kitchen window as well as the boulevard in front of the house, absolutely deserted. They had seen Clement go by, who had greeted them in passing; then, two minutes later, M. Allou's housekeeper, whom they knew well.

Shortly thereafter she returned to tell them breathlessly that the door of the flat was locked on the inside and nobody was answering their knocks. They ran there immediately and found Clement standing in the vestibule. He motioned to them to guard the door, adding that the murderer was certainly still in the house.

The officers had certainly believed him, because they had heard M. Allou's shout and the shot when they were no more than ten metres from the corner of the boulevard; and they had met nobody on the way in. Furthermore, it was impossible for anyone to have jumped from the second floor.

'That's true,' I said, 'but if the assailant didn't come down the stairs, he could have gone up. It's a pity you didn't search the third floor right away. Now, with the crowd swarming the staircase, it's too late; he wouldn't have waited for us....'

'But,' replied one of the officers, 'Clement never left the spot...'

'And who's to say,' I retorted, 'that he didn't let the murderer leave?'

In any case, it appeared from the evidence that Clement was either the culprit or his accomplice. I gave the order to have him searched.

They didn't find the famous wallet on him, nor any weapon. But in an inside pocket of his jacket they found twenty one-thousand franc notes.

Twenty-thousand francs! Exactly what had been found on the vagrant....

'Well, there seems to be a standard fee!' I murmured.

'Oh, Your Honour, how could you believe...' stammered Clement. 'It's monstrous...I'm an honest man....'

'So can you tell me where this money comes from?'

'They're my savings.'

'They're quite sizeable; and do you always carry them around on your person?'

'Yes, I'm afraid to leave the money at home. I'm away too much.'

'Come, come, don't play me for a fool!'

'But, Your Honour, you didn't find a wallet or a gun on me...'

'You know perfectly well there was a crowd in the flat not long ago, when the doctor arrived. You could have given anything you wanted to an accomplice!'

'But how would I have had time to break into the desk?'

'More than a minute elapsed, according to witnesses and your own account, between the revolver shot and the arrival of the officers. Look at how ham-fisted the break-in was; it was obviously someone in a hurry, for whom a minute would have been ample time....'

'That's true,' acknowledged Clement.

'So the twenty-thousand francs are not your savings at all, but either payment for the crime you committed, or the price of your silence if you'd let the culprit go before the police arrived. It's one or the other. Admit it!'

Clement hung his head.

'It's true that everything points to me,' he said, 'Luckily, M. Allou is not dead. As soon as he recovers, he'll tell you what happened!'

'I hope as much as you do that he'll recover. Meanwhile, can you explain to me what you did in the minute you were left alone, since you claim you didn't break into the desk?'

'I didn't move, Your Honour...I thought the killer was still there, that he was about to pounce on me...I didn't dare move...If I'd stepped away from the door, he could have got away...or attacked me from behind....'

'You have an answer for everything,' I noted drily. 'The jury will appreciate that. Clement, I charge you with premeditated murder.'

And, while the officers were taking him away, the inspector shouted:

'But why would I have done all that, Your Honour, why?'

Yes, why? That was the heart of the mystery; the rest was simple.

I could think of only one explanation: Pierre Louret's revenge, for which the inspector was the perpetrator or the accomplice.

CHAPTER XII

SURPRISES

Without even stopping for lunch, I rushed to the hospital. The surgeon had already examined the victim. He planned to go ahead with a trepanning, in order to remove the bullet, which the radiography had located precisely.

The specialist was reasonably optimistic. Obviously, he dared not guarantee anything about such a delicate operation; but there were, he assured me, considerable grounds for hope.

Any interrogation of the wounded man was out of the question for the moment. He had not yet regained consciousness. And even when he had recovered, it would be necessary to avoid tiring him.

All that the surgeon could tell me with any precision was the trajectory of the bullet. As I had already guessed, he concluded that the shot had been fired at a distance of more than fifty centimetres (beyond that, it was not possible to be more precise), from behind, in a perfectly horizontal direction and very slightly from right to left. Accident or suicide could be ruled out completely.

Another half-millimetre and the shot would have been fatal.

I left, after receiving a promise to be kept informed of my colleague's progress by telephone. As I was leaving I ran into several magistrates who, like me, had come to learn the latest news. I noticed that opinions about the crime were divided: some believed Clement guilty of the crime; others felt that he was implicated in the escape of the culprit. But all were lost when it came to the motive.

After a very rapid lunch, I returned to my chambers. There, I found Chief Superintendent Dumas who had been notified by telegraph and had left Marseilles by car immediately.

He observed that his predictions had been accurate and the affair had turned out to be much more complex than anyone had imagined. I had to acknowledge his foresight.

'I don't believe,' he added, 'in the kind of truth that leaps out at you from a dossier…I have too much experience not to know that we earn our bread by the sweat of our brow! Believe me, Your Honour, the hardest work has yet to come.'

Then he briefed me on the results of the laboratory fingerprint tests.

On the truncheon which had been used to kill Louret senior, the traces were too faint and too blurred to draw any conclusions.

And the dagger used to kill William was clean of prints. The murderer had taken care to wear gloves or carry a handkerchief.

The other dagger, however—the one found beside the body of Gaston Richaud—provided more evidence. Pierre Louret's fingerprints (which had been taken the day before, when he arrived in jail) were perfectly visible.

M. Allou's deductions on this point were therefore confirmed.

Then we talked about the most recent murder attempt and the two alternative theories.

'Revenge on the part of Pierre Louret...' mused Dumas. 'You know, criminals never bear grudges against judges. That's an observation that I personally have made a hundred times, and which is generally recognised....'

'So we should reject that theory?' I asked.

'I wouldn't go that far...Pierre Louret may have had another reason for taking revenge on M. Allou...I don't want to say any more...In any case, it's clear that Clement has been the agent or the accomplice. I was suspicious of him all along; you see that my instincts were right!'

Neither Dumas nor I could understand why Clement was continuing to deny his involvement.

'There's another obscure aspect,' I observed. 'Why, after the housekeeper had left, did M. Allou lock the door; and why didn't he respond to the ringing of the doorbell? Can't we conclude that, by the time the housekeeper arrived, the killer had already got in and had locked the door? Clement was only in front of the door as a lookout. That would confirm he was an accomplice.'

'Not necessarily,' replied the chief superintendent. 'M. Allou could have seen Clement from his window. Not wanting to meet him, for one reason or another, he locked the door and didn't answer the bell. That would explain why he only shouted for help when Clement started to break down the door...And also, you see, it increases the likelihood of Clement's direct involvement.'

'Unless,' I countered, 'the killer got in before Clement and bound and gagged M. Allou; and he only worked himself loose after the housekeeper had left. That would mean that Clement broke down the door to help his accomplice....'

Dumas acknowledged the validity of my argument.

Meanwhile, the latest news had thrown the good citizens of Aix into a paroxysm of fear. The series of baffling crimes at Puyricard had sent an enormous shock wave throughout the whole of France; and now, suddenly the affair had been brought into Aix itself, and under even more mysterious circumstances.

Reporters from Paris and Marseilles, whom I had been able to hold at bay at Cypress Villa, were circling me now—I could sense it—waiting outside the door of my chambers, ready to ask me what I was going to do. What should I tell them?

I shared my concerns with Dumas, who replied:

'Don't say anything about a conspiracy theory. Say that you've arrested the culprit and that's the end of it; what more can anyone ask? As for Pierre Louret, say that he is being sought everywhere, and his arrest is imminent. With such an assurance, delivered in an authoritative manner, you will calm the first emotional reactions. Interest will dwindle day by day, and in a month, almost nobody will be talking about him…All that's left then will be to insinuate that he's been killed by his accomplices and divert attention back to Clement.'

'Yes, I can see you have a great deal of experience of this sort of thing…But do you really think we will never find Pierre Louret?'

'He's very cunning,' replied Dumas, 'and, what's more important, he seems to be part of a remarkably well-organised gang. Look how well his escape was carried out. They had no way of knowing that you would send for Pierre Louret so quickly. There must therefore have been someone stationed full-time in the main hall of the *Palais de Justice.* As soon as the accused arrived, he notified his accomplices; and they stole a lawyer's car that they knew would be there until midday. Now, with the money Louret now has….'

'Has he actually received his inheritance? I'd completely forgotten to check that,' I exclaimed. 'These constant shocks are causing me to lose track.'

Immediately I asked that the president of the Avignon Bar Association be put on the line urgently. He was able to provide me with the name of the colleague, Maitre Rissou, who handled the Maurat estate; the matter had caused enough of a stir for the respectable lawyer to have become quite famous in the region.

I reached him straight away. He informed me that, on Maurat's death, his entire fortune, almost all in real estate, had been placed in a strong-box in one of the banks. Pierre Louret had waited a week before liquidating everything. The will was a formality: the solicitor had known for a long time that there was no protected heir, so Louret had had no difficulty.

He had obtained a proxy from his sister to divide the estate; it was done immediately and Pierre Louret had taken what was due to him. What had he done with it? The solicitor didn't know.

The young man had demanded, very aggressively, to take charge of his sister's part as well. But the solicitor pointed out that the proxy applied only to the division of the inheritance and not its release, which he refused to do without formal authorisation. Pierre Louret had gone away furious.

A few days later, Maitre Rissou had written to the young woman to request her instructions but she had died the day before. Fifteen million francs were therefore in the hands of the solicitor—or, more accurately, in a safe in the Bank of France—the key to which had been given to the public prosecutor as soon as he had learned of Pierre Louret's arrest that morning.

He was unaware of Louret's escape, to which he reacted fearfully, not troubling to hide it.

Throughout the phone conversation, Dumas had been listening on an earphone.

'You see,' he said to me as he hung up, 'Louret has fifteen million at his disposal. He'll know how to use it...We're never going to find him! Unless....'

'Unless?...'

'...Clement decides to talk!'

There was a knock at the door of my chambers, which my clerk went to open. There followed a short discussion and he returned to inform me that a tradesman, M. Daniel, had something interesting to tell me.

I had him brought in immediately, and Dumas introduced us; he had, in fact, known the fellow for a number of years and it appeared that Daniel had supplied him with useful information from time to time.

The man had been running one of the town's principal cafés for over twenty-five years, and was in a good position to learn things.

'What I saw last night,' he said, 'is maybe of no interest. However, as soon as I heard the rumours about Clement's arrest, I thought I should report it, just in case.'

He explained that the café closed at half past midnight and that every night he crossed the town to get back home. The previous night, as he was walking back, he noticed Clement in a small, little-used back street, talking to someone.

It was a dark night but he had definitely recognised the inspector, who visited the café every day, and with whom he was on good terms. But he didn't think Clement had seen him.

As for the person he was talking to, Daniel could not give us a precise description. From a distance, he could only say that the individual, who was small and thin, appeared to be very young, possibly not yet twenty.

'Ah!' exclaimed Dumas, 'that description exactly fits the individual I noticed by M. Allou's door and who made a sign to Clement. That's why he left us so soon—at midnight—after we left your colleague's house! Continue, M. Daniel, continue, all this is very interesting. You said it was around half past midnight?'

'Twelve forty, in fact. When I noticed Clement, I must admit I had the idea of going over to him, just to satisfy my curiosity. All anyone was talking about in town was the arrest of Pierre Louret, but nobody knew how he'd managed to pull off his mysterious deeds.

'So I waited until they'd finished their conversation. Not very patiently, because it had started to rain. I took shelter under a porch, and that's probably why neither of them saw me. The discussion lasted a good ten minutes longer. Then I saw the other fellow hand Clement a small package which he put into his inside jacket pocket.'

'A small package,' I interrupted. 'Could it have been, for example, bank notes?'

'Yes, very easily. A bundle of notes would have been about that size.'

'Perfect. Continue.'

'There's not much more to say. The other fellow went off, and I walked over to meet Clement. But he pretended not to see me and turned sharply into a cross-street. He strode off and I didn't dare follow him.'

'You said that you knew Clement quite well,' said Dumas. 'In your opinion what's his character: what kind of morals does he have? What's he capable of?'

Daniel thought for a few seconds and replied:

'One thing struck me, and it's what all of his friends say about him: his greed. I always felt you could get him to do almost anything for money.'

M. Daniel left as soon as the clerk had transcribed his testimony. Dumas immediately gave the order to his men to find the mysterious other person; I could tell there and then that the effort was doomed to failure, for the description was too vague.

That evening, I went to the hospital. They confirmed what I had been told over the phone. The operation had been successful and the small—6 mm x 35—bullet had been removed. The patient had not regained consciousness.

By eight o'clock the next day I was at my desk. A remarkable surprise awaited me.

Thumbing through the mail from the last delivery, one of the envelopes caught my attention. Someone had cut out a number of phrases from the previous day's newspaper: "examining magistrate," "Aix-en-Provence" and "strictly personal," and used them to form the address. And the subject: "The Pierre Louret proceedings…."

With considerable trepidation I opened the envelope. The letter, as I had expected, was created in the same way and read simply:

"You know my power and my determination. If you do not release Clement, you will suffer the same fate as your colleague. And I do not miss my victims."

It was not signed, but I immediately suspected Pierre Louret.

'This is too much!' I exclaimed. 'What a fool! Who does he take me for? He's condemning his accomplice while trying to save him!'

I telephoned the prison straight away, to find out if Clement had named a lawyer, for I could only interrogate him with one there. The governor told me the accused had said he did not need a lawyer; that his innocence would become apparent as soon as M. Allou could speak; and that he asked nothing more than to be questioned right away.

In order to avoid another escape like that of the previous day, I went to the prison myself, and took my clerk along.

Clement soon appeared in the visiting room. I asked him point-blank:

'Who were you talking to last night in Rifle-Rafle Street?'

His face twitched.

'I didn't talk to anyone,' he replied, 'I went straight home.'

'Someone saw you, however….'

'Your Honour, there are always snitches that will tell any story to get a payout from the police. May I ask the name of this witness?'

'Certainly, he's never asked to keep it secret. It's Daniel.'

Clement shrugged his shoulders:

'Daniel? He's a professional informer.'

'Maybe; that doesn't mean he's lying.'
'You'll find out he's lying once M. Allou is able to speak!'
'That's not all,' I continued. 'Your accomplice Louret has betrayed you by trying to defend you.'
Clement went pale and stammered:
'He's betrayed me?'
'Yes, he's officially denounced you.'
'It's not possible,' muttered Clement. (His knees started to buckle and he had to sit down.) 'It's not possible...Louret isn't my accomplice...I don't understand anything about these set-ups....'
'Read this!' I said.
And I handed him the letter.
'It's scary,' he stammered. 'I don't know who's got it in for me. If M. Allou had died, I would have been finished! But he'll pull through, won't he? He'll pull through?'
I left without having obtained any sort of confession.

At the *Palais de Justice*, I was told that my colleague's condition had improved, and that he had uttered a few words. I left as soon as I heard this and went straight to the hospital, accompanied by my clerk, in case there was any testimony to be taken down.
On the way I met Dumas, who decided to come along with me.
'If he regains consciousness,' I said to the chief superintendent, 'we'll have the solution.'
'I don't think so,' grunted Dumas, enigmatically.
We reached the hospital and, through a maze of corridors and staircases—the hospital at Aix is a very old building—we were led to a small room. M. Allou was lying there, very pale, his features drawn; his head was heavily bandaged. As I approached, I saw his eyelids flicker.
'Can you hear me?' I asked.
He opened his eyes and appeared to recognise us. Then, slowly, he started to speak:
'I was hit as I was at the door, opening it. I fell down; I didn't see anything....'
'But no,' I told him, 'you were hit when you were at the window, and that's where you fell down. Mlle. Escoiffier heard the sound of the fall right above her head!'
His eyes wavered, but he repeated:
'No, in front of the door, when I opened it. I don't know who it was...A man....'

And he lapsed into unconsciousness.

'Leave him now,' said the doctor.

And he followed us into the corridor.

'Alas!' I said, 'My poor friend's mind is wandering. He doesn't even remember the spot where he was wounded....'

The doctor's manner was grave.

'I'm reasonably confident that he'll live,' he said, 'but I can't speak to his mind. After a wound and an operation like that, it's possible he'll never recover his reason.'

I left with a heavy heart.

'We're never going to find out more,' said Dumas.

'No!' I protested. 'I refuse to believe that such a fine intellect will be lost forever.'

'I said,' retorted Dumas, 'that we're never going to find out more.'

At two o'clock I returned to my chambers. I had no intention, at least for a while, to spend any more time on this infamous case. It was up to the police to find Pierre Louret; at this point, my involvement had ended. So many of the other judicial matters had been delayed that I didn't begrudge devoting some time to them.

But, as fate would have it, my other projects would, once again, be turned upside-down by new surprises! In my mail, I found the following letter:

"Pierre Louret is at Pont-de-l'Arc, at Chateau Bastoux."

No signature. The handwriting was deliberately devoid of personal characteristics.

I sat there confused... I had the distinct impression of being the victim of a bad joke. Who would know so much about the case? Who would benefit from unmasking the criminal?

Nevertheless, this case had been so full of surprises that I could not afford to be sceptical. Better to be thought a dupe than to overlook the slightest chance.

I therefore dutifully phoned Dumas, who had just returned to Marseilles.

'I don't believe a word of it,' he said. 'There are always people amusing themselves at our expense. But I'll come over anyway.'

An hour later, he was back.

'Before we risk scorn and ridicule by unleashing a military-style operation,' he explained, 'we need to check this out; we may find it's just decent folk who are scared stiff. So I've sent over two inspectors, both very discreet and very capable, and they'll report back on their local enquiries in short order.'

Pont-de-l'Arc is a small hamlet situated about a kilometre from Aix, in the direction of Marseilles. It wouldn't be a long wait.

They arrived around four o'clock, and told us the following:

The property known pompously as "Chateau Bastoux" was a square old house standing in complete isolation eight hundred metres from the hamlet. It was set in woods where pine, broom, and spiny oak surrounded it in a dense thicket.

The owner, a thoroughly upstanding individual who owned a tobacco shop, had rented the house two years earlier to people from outside the region. He didn't know much about his tenants, although, —to judge from the comings and goings—there must have been five or six of them living there. It wasn't possible for him to be more precise, because there were three roads leading to the property, only one of which went past his own home.

'There might be something to this,' murmured Dumas.

'It's too late to conduct a search today,' I remarked,'The sun's down and it would be illegal. Besides, there are precautions to be taken. Are you sure,' I asked the inspectors, 'that you haven't alerted anyone by your enquiries?'

They assured me that was not the case. They had posed as brokers, looking for a place to rent, and had only spoken to the owner. He was so garrulous that they had hardly needed to ask him any questions; and there were no witnesses to the conversation.

I decided to launch the operation at sunrise the next day.

The police captain came to discuss his plan with us. In the early morning, he would deploy his men to surround the house at a distance of five hundred metres, so that they would not be heard, even by any dogs. It would be simple for them to hide in the thicket. If Pierre Louret tried to escape, he would not be able to slip through the net.

I was going to conduct the search myself, accompanied by Chief Superintendent Dumas, ten inspectors, and five *gendarmes*.

For now, only Dumas, the captain, and myself were aware of the plan. It had been agreed that the others would only be briefed at the last minute.

I returned home somewhat uneasy, I have to admit. The threat contained in the first letter was still on my mind and I kept my hand on the revolver in my pocket; I kept away from any suspicious passer-by.

Before going to sleep, I inspected my small flat very thoroughly, wishing the locks were more solid.

I thought about the next day's expedition. Would we be greeted with revolver shots? Or, more likely, would we find honest upright citizens, furious at the farcical proceedings?

CHAPTER XIII

SEARCH

A quarter of an hour before sunrise, I was with Dumas at Pont-de-l'Arc. The police captain joined us to inform us that the house was entirely surrounded and that he personally guaranteed there was no possibility of escape.

Our auxiliary personnel having arrived, we set off. The sky was clear and there was a brisk chill in the air.

Three hundred metres from the hamlet we left the main road to take a wide path to our left. Shortly after, we arrived under the pines, where it was still quite dark. But I could make out several uniforms between the clusters of oaks, which was reassuring.

Besides, the sun was starting to rise.

Five minutes later we arrived in front of the house; the five *gendarmes* who accompanied us quickly spread out to encircle it. The shutters were closed and everybody inside appeared to be asleep. That did not surprise me, given that no dogs had howled at our approach.

I went up the two old stone steps leading to the front door; a rusty chain was hanging there, which I pulled hard. A bell rang.

The piercing noise, in the silence of a winter morning, had something menacing about it that chilled me to the bone, and my heart started to pound. I have to confess that I flattened myself instinctively against the wall, as if someone was going to fire on me through the door.

Nothing moved…I rang a second time.

Then a shutter opened on the first floor and a man's voice asked:

'What do you want?'

'Open in the name of the law!' I replied. 'This is a search!'

'I'm coming down,' the voice replied.

A few minutes later the door opened, revealing a man in his fifties, of medium height but broad-shouldered; a hooked nose dominated a clean-shaven, somewhat fleshy, face.

'What's this about, gentlemen?' he said in a calm voice.

At the same time, the ten inspectors went into the house and started their methodical search. As the house was not very big, the operation was not expected to take long.

Four other individuals, all men, were woken up and sent, in pyjamas or dressing-gowns, into the lounge; there, despite their scanty clothing, they were thoroughly searched. Revolver in hand, Dumas and one of the inspectors monitored them.

We obliged the fellow who had opened the door to join the others and he continued to repeat in his calm voice:

'I have no idea what you're doing, gentlemen. And I hope to receive an apology later. We're honest businessmen from Marseilles who have come here to hunt, and I fail to understand why we're being treated like highwaymen!'

The words and the manner made some impression on me. Were we all victims of a diversion? If that was the case, with the size of the force I had deployed, I was going to cover myself in ridicule!

The search went on…It seemed to me that we had been there for hours…I knew already that nothing had been found in the rooms or the cupboards; heavy blows told me that they were now tapping the walls, looking for secret passages or hiding places.

Then the inspectors returned.

'There's nothing,' they said, 'absolutely nothing. We checked everything.'

Dumas and I looked at each other in consternation.

'This is a very regrettable error,' announced the fellow who had opened the door. 'We have no doubt been the victims of a joke in very bad taste; nevertheless I am amazed that it was taken at face value, considering the good reputation of the people involved.'

I was about to respond and offer my excuses when I heard, quite distinctly, a revolver shot outside…And I saw the man go suddenly pale!

I was outside straight away, leaving the occupants of the house under the capable eyes of the inspectors. For several minutes, I saw nothing. Then, on the approach road to the house, I saw a *gendarme* running towards me. As I went to meet him he announced:

'Pierre Louret has just been killed!'

'What!' I exclaimed. 'You couldn't take him alive?'

'It wasn't us,' answered the *gendarme*. 'I don't understand what happened…I'll explain.'

'Later,' I replied.

So saying, I ran back to the house. I was anxious to exploit what had happened.

'Pierre Louret has been captured,' I announced as I entered the lounge, 'and he's told us everything.'

'In that case,' replied the man, who appeared to be the leader of the group, 'we're done for. I'm not going to be so stupid as to argue. He was indeed one of us.'

The inspectors immediately seized and handcuffed everyone present.

To tell the truth, this sudden frankness left me somewhat suspicious. It seemed as if it was aimed at concealing other secrets. But, for the moment, I couldn't afford to question anyone further, in case they realised, from my questions, that Louret had not spoken.

'Take them to Aix,' I ordered, 'and lock them up in absolute secrecy.'

Once they had left I had the *gendarme* brought in and asked him what had happened. This is what he explained:

He had been hiding with one of his colleagues in the bushes. Suddenly they saw Louret stand up a hundred metres in front of them. Up until then, he had probably been crawling through the thicket.

Then he leapt forward in their direction; they decided to lie low and catch him as he was going past. But hardly had Louret gone two metres before a shot rang out from behind a dense bush and he crashed to the ground.

The *gendarmes* rushed towards the body, where they realised he'd been shot in the head and had died on the spot.

But the hundred metres they'd had to cover, plus the cursory examination, had taken several minutes. By the time they reached the bush there was nobody there. And any further search of the thicket would be extremely difficult.

Suddenly they heard the sound of a motorcycle departing in the distance. That was all.

But two other *gendarmes* came forward. They told me that the motorcycle had gone right by them on a narrow path. They had just been able to get a glimpse of the rider: a young man of sixteen or thereabouts, in blue mechanic's overalls. But they hadn't had time to stop him and had fired too late as he sped away at an incredible speed.

I stood there, dumbfounded. At every step the mystery deepened. Now Pierre Louret, the culprit, had suddenly become the victim.

There was nothing more to be done there. I left several men behind with instructions to guard the house. Then I left with the chief superintendent, who remained silent.

I, on the other hand, felt an irrepressible urge to speak. At one point, I made the following observation:

'Look here, M. Dumas, we have to admit in all honesty that what happened here is beyond our comprehension. If only M. Allou were here! Without him, we'll never work it out!'

Dumas glowered at me and murmured:

'I admire your enthusiasm!'

Fully understanding his attitude, I didn't press the matter. In spite of him I had the utmost confidence in M. Allou.

And as soon as we reached Aix I rushed to the hospital.

CHAPTER XIV

THE CONFESSION

Upon my arrival I was agreeably struck by the doctor's smile.

'I believe our patient is saved,' he said happily, 'and his reason also! Since this morning he has completely regained consciousness and now talks like you and me. Not the slightest sign of any mental problem. See for yourself....'

As soon as I walked into the room I recognised the attentive look of the old M. Allou, decisive and somewhat intimidating at the same time. He was propped up by two pillows; on a table I saw a bowl and the remains of several bananas, which I found most encouraging.

'Well, my dear colleague, I've come back from afar,' he said to me in a contented voice. 'I'm sorry, but I couldn't return to duty as soon as I'd promised. Not only that but I'm the cause of a whole new case! Forgive me, it's not my fault....'

We spoke for a few minutes about his health. But I was keen to get to the topic which interested me.

'Now tell me,' I said, 'exactly what happened to you.'

'But I don't know anything at all, my poor friend. And I was counting on you to tell me. There's very little I can tell you.

'Still, here goes. I was sleeping peacefully because the previous day had been very tiring and we had all gone to bed very late. Suddenly, someone rang the doorbell and I woke up. It was already daytime and I looked at my watch, which showed nine thirty.'

'Your watch had almost certainly stopped,' I interrupted.

'Perhaps. It's easy to check; if it hasn't been wound since, it will still show nine thirty.'

'Unfortunately,' I said, 'your housekeeper couldn't find it. I think it may have been stolen when the crowd rushed into the flat after the doctor arrived.'

'That's bad news,' replied M. Allou. 'That won't help the investigation. All the same, I don't believe my watch stopped. I wind it every morning; if I'd forgotten to do so the day before, it would have stopped during the daytime and I would have noticed.'

'Although,' I observed, 'if you'd wound it very early the previous day, it wouldn't be surprising if it were stopped at nine thirty.'

'Perhaps. As I was saying, someone rang and I thought my housekeeper would answer. After a short while, they rang again, more persistently. Thinking that the housekeeper might be at the market, I put on my dressing-gown and went to see. But no sooner had I turned the latch—.'

'Latch or bolt?' I interrupted.

'Latch. I had no reason to bolt the door that night. So I had scarcely turned the latch and started to open the door, when it was pushed forcefully. I glimpsed the silhouette of a man just before I received a hard blow to the head. That's all I remember; I must have lost consciousness.'

'That's very curious,' I replied. 'What I saw doesn't match your account at all. The door had been smashed, the bolt was still shut and you'd been shot in the head in front of the bedroom window!'

'Yes, it's certainly strange. I can assure you that nobody broke the door down, because I opened it myself. I can still see it in my mind's eye....'

I was starting to become irritated. Once again, I was getting the feeling that M. Allou was trying to mislead us. But why give such an unlikely version? Someone as intelligent as he should be able to create a better story....

We both remained silent for several minutes, then M. Allou continued:

'I understand you've arrested poor Clement...I don't think he's got anything to do with the case. I'm afraid he's just jinxed.

'I was also told that the good Mlle. Escoiffier had heard me opening the window and shouting for help. She's an honest witness and lacking imagination, so her testimony is worrisome, I realise...So worrisome, in fact, that I have—how to say this? a vague, a very vague memory of doing that...like something I did in a previous existence...Come, my young colleague, tell me everything you know. Open up the dossier orally for me. That's often how I get to the truth.'

I had a second's hesitation. But the funny thing was, once I started, my confidence returned. And I gave M. Allou a very detailed account of everything that had happened.

When I came to the anonymous letter, which I had attributed to Pierre Louret, my colleague smiled with a mocking glint in his eye.

'I applaud your courage,' he said, 'but not your perspicacity. How could you have believed that the letter came from Pierre Louret?'

'Well....'

'Why would he have taken the trouble to paste letters cut from a newspaper? So what, if we recognised his handwriting?'

'That's true,' I murmured. 'I'm an idiot!'

'No,' replied M. Allou indulgently, 'you were distraught, that's all. Besides, how could I criticise you when my own thinking has been so shallow? Yes, I was so confident that my explanations were sufficient, that there was nothing left to find out. It all seemed so coherent, so logical…I truly thought the case was finished.

'That was only partly true. I lacked judgment. I did not foresee that there was a complete organisation, and that they would arrange for his escape for fear of what he might reveal….'

'Quite so,' I observed, 'If he had remained in our hands, he could have told us a lot of interesting things. He told me, as he was leaving my chambers, that he might talk… later…If they'd abandoned him, he was prepared to avenge himself.'

'Yes,' continued M. Allou, 'and they sprang him right away. But continue with your account, I'm beginning to see an explanation….'

'What is it?' I exclaimed.

'Continue, continue. So far, it's only a hypothesis. It will only be born out if we suddenly learn of the murder of Pierre Louret himself….'

'But it's true!' I exclaimed. 'I was going to tell you, he's just been killed!'

'How?' he asked.

'A revolver shot.'

'Naturally, nobody has been arrested?'

'No, but somebody was seen!'

'Before anything else,' continued M. Allou, 'where's the body?'

'I've had it brought here for the autopsy.'

My colleague asked me to arrange for a surgeon immediately, in order to extract the bullet that had killed Louret and compare it with the one that had wounded him. It's known, in fact, that each gun barrel has its own unique characteristics, faults in the metal, which score the bullet; hence the bullet bears the mark of the weapon that fired it, which can be scientifically recognised.

While the surgeon was operating, I dispatched my clerk to look for the bullet which had hit M. Allou, and simultaneously sent for the town's leading firearms expert. After a microscopic examination of the two projectiles, he concluded officially that they had been fired from the same weapon.

I reported this finding to M. Allou immediately, and his expression brightened.

'Perfect,' he said. 'My theory has been confirmed. But continue your account from the point where you left off.'

When I started to talk about the motorcyclist, M. Allou interrupted:

'Did anyone get a good look at him?'

'No, just the silhouette; someone in blue mechanic's overalls....'

'...and apparently fifteen or sixteen years old,' finished M. Allou.

I stood there dumbfounded, and managed to blurt out:

'Why, yes. Exactly. That's quite extraordinary ...How did you know?'

My colleague smiled:

'It's only a hypothesis,' he said. 'But it's starting to look pretty close to the mark. We're going to try and settle the matter, if you agree. After all, there's no harm in trying, and upon my word, I think it'll work...Tonight, with the co-operation of the doctor here, you will officially announce my death to all the newspapers.'

'Why?' I asked.

But without answering my question M. Allou continued:

'Not before eleven o'clock, still in time for the morning editions. At that hour, everyone is asleep, so there'll be no-one to contradict the story. I will undertake, between now and this evening, to progressively exacerbate my condition!'

'I'll do what you want,' I said, 'even though it looks very risky!'

'No doubt, but it's the only way to save Clement.'

'What!' I exclaimed in astonishment. 'Don't you think Clement has played a major role in this business? Either he fired at you, or he let the culprit escape!'

'How do you arrive at that definitive conclusion?' asked M. Allou, smiling once again.

His mocking attitude annoyed me.

'I don't imagine,' I replied somewhat tersely, 'that you could have been wounded in your own flat if there hadn't been anyone there? Because the direction of the bullet ruled out accident or suicide!'

'You don't imagine...' replied M. Allou, his smile widening. 'Must Clement be the victim of your lack of imagination?'

I said nothing and he continued:

'So follow my instructions to the letter!'

'And afterwards,' I asked, 'what should I do?'

'Afterwards? Why, go to bed, if you're the serious young man that I hope you are. Be at your chambers at eight in the morning tomorrow and wait...Everything comes to him who waits....'

'But...What about this afternoon?...'

'Take care of matters that you have let slide; there must be quite a few, I would think? You'll never get through your work, my young colleague, if you keep leaving your chambers on the slightest pretext. You are confusing the legal process with the detective novel....'

'But,' I retorted, somewhat vexed, 'you yourself came out to meet me the other day at Cypress Villa.'

'Only in order to rescue you, otherwise you would have been stuck there until your retirement...But there was nothing I learned that I couldn't have found out from my chambers, and nothing was done that I could not have ordered from there.'

'But,' I protested, 'you often visit crime scenes.'

'Of course it is sometimes unavoidable to get a clear idea of the layout when it's relevant; but, once you have what you need, go back to your chambers and think! Your chosen profession of examining magistrate consists, above all, of reflection, my young colleague... Don't be cross with me; it's experience that pays off over the years and it's the highest value a man can put on anything...I would prefer, believe me, to be in your shoes rather than mine; what counts is not what you have, but what you will have....'

On those words I left M. Allou, a little starry-eyed....

Then the doctor and I proceeded to organise the scenario that he wanted, of which I understood absolutely nothing. We arranged that, until the evening, nobody would go into my colleague's room except a harmless male nurse incapable of judging the real state of his health. No external visitors were allowed.

Then, following his advice, I went to my chambers to finish the backlog of work which had accumulated so disturbingly.

When I left, around six o'clock, the rumour was already rife in town that M. Allou's condition was deteriorating minute by minute. At eight o'clock, several people assured me that the unfortunate magistrate would not last the night...So everything was going according to plan.

By ten o'clock, I was back in the hospital. In the entrance lobby several journalists were waiting for news and I pretended I was going to find out. I went into M. Allou's room, where the nurse was standing watch; I offered to take his place for a while, if he wanted to catch some sleep. He was only too delighted to accept; that allowed me to talk to my colleague—who seemed in even better shape than in the morning—and the doctor, who joined us shortly afterwards.

Then, as eleven o'clock approached, I went back down to the vestibule, taking care to keep a look of consternation on my face.

'Is he dead?' asked the journalists immediately.

By way of response I made a broad gesture which could have meant anything, but which was interpreted as confirmation. The journalists, after a few motionless moments of silence and a posture of sadness befitting the occasion, hurried off in search of telephones.

Thus I had contrived not to tell an untruth and my responsibility, the next day, would be to lie low. I went off to bed.

Needless to say I didn't sleep much. By seven o'clock the next morning, I was to be found wandering around town, feverishly impatient. The headlines of the newspaper I had bought said, in big letters:

'Pierre Louret mysteriously killed. M. Allou succumbs to his wounds.'

I attempted to read further, for the sake of something to do, but I couldn't manage to stay focused…One thought drove out all others: what would I learn this morning? What was M. Allou's theory?

At five minutes to eight, I reached the *Palais de Justice*. And, on the first floor, in front of the door to my chambers, I saw a young woman waiting for me…A small brunette, very pretty, I must say; and maybe twenty years old at most.

She came towards me:

'The examining magistrate?'

'At your service, mademoiselle. How can I be of assistance?'

My smile froze before the implacable stare of the young woman; this was clearly not the moment to start flirting with her.

'I need to talk to you,' she replied coldly.

And we went into my chambers, where my clerk had preceded us a few moments earlier.

Hardly had I sat down and indicated an armchair to my strange visitor when, disregarding my gesture, she said, looking me straight in the eye:

'It was I who killed M. Allou.'

I was out of my chair in one bound!

'And it was I who killed Pierre Louret as well.'

I stood thunderstruck for several seconds, with the strange feeling that I was hallucinating….

'But who are you?' I managed to get out at last.

She raised her chin proudly:

'I am the mistress of Gaston Richaud, the cousin of Pierre Louret!'

And she suddenly collapsed into an armchair, bursting into tears. I heard a confused jumble of words:

'It makes no difference now. Do what you like...kill me...I don't care any more...it's all the same to me. He's been avenged!'

Little by little she calmed down and had no difficulty giving me her confession.

'My lover,' she said, 'was not, I must confess, an honest man. That didn't bother me because I loved him; even if he'd been a hundred times more guilty, I would still have loved him as much. Even so, I would have preferred him to be honest; I myself would never steal, sir; I'm Corsican, I know how to take my revenge, but I've never committed an act that my conscience would not allow.

'What did Gaston Richaud do in life? What does it matter to you? He's dead, he's paid his dues. But he always acted alone, you know: he never wanted to be part of an organisation like his cousin Pierre Louret. Alas! If he had been, he'd be alive today; Louret would never have dared to kill him....'

'Which gang was it?' I asked.

'That I don't know, sir. Pierre Louret came to see his cousin quite often; together, they had even organised....'

She hesitated, and I completed the sentence:

'Crimes?'

'Yes, crimes...It doesn't matter, they're both dead! Louret spoke freely in front of me. I often heard him insist that my lover become a member of his organisation. Several times, in fact, he came to see us accompanied by a man who appeared to rank higher than him in the gang and who tried to persuade us in the same way.'

'And why did Richaud refuse to join?'

'He told me that they paid him a higher price for his poisons as long as he stayed independent and wasn't obliged to supply them. One day, about two months ago, Pierre Louret came to visit us and proposed that he and my friend murder their uncle Maurat; he pretended he knew the will said the fortune would be divided into three equal parts; it was a lie, as you know.

'Gaston accepted. We discussed the choice of poison for quite a while. Then we decided on the one you know and coated the knife blade with it.'

While she was talking I looked for the knife among the police exhibits. The young woman took it, examined it, and placed it back on the table.

'Yes, that's it,' she said, 'I recognise it. You know how the murder took place; Pierre Louret killed his uncle during a walk in the country; death was instantaneous.

'Gaston went to the burial, where his cousin told him that the will had not yet been read; that if they appeared too keen to have it done, they would appear suspect; and that, as soon as the solicitor was ready, he would be notified.

'Do you want to know what I think, Your Honour? Louret hoped that the solicitor would turn over not just his part, but also his sister's. And then he would have disappeared forever.'

'Yes, mademoiselle, I believe your theory is correct. He did indeed try to take possession of all the money. But he came up against the solicitor's prudence.'

'I thought as much,' she continued. 'That was also Gaston's opinion, which he repeated to me the day before he died. You didn't know Germaine Louret; she was a very cautious and pathologically fearful person; that's why she was so careful with the proxy. It seems obvious to me that once she took possession of her share, her brother wouldn't be able to steal it; she would take steps to shelter it. So he resorted to crime.

'Several weeks passed after Maurat's death and Gaston had still not received any word about the will. That's when I went with him to Avignon on his motorcycle to learn more. There, he found out the truth and flew into an uncontrollable rage. In spite of all my pleas, because I feared a tragedy, he decided to go to Aix immediately to force his cousin to explain himself. And so we set out, still on his motorcycle.

'You know the rest. What M. Allou worked out is entirely correct. We stopped in Aix, where he went straight away to Cypress Villa; while I was waiting for him, I learned about Germaine Louret having been murdered the night before. But Gaston didn't know that until he returned. He understood then why the house had been under surveillance; why, when he had sent out his customary signal that night, he had been grabbed by a man whom he had killed without hesitation. He had not known it was William, who had been kind to him when he had spent a few months at the villa. But what could he have done? He couldn't afford to be caught prowling around the house: he would have been suspected of complicity in the Maurat murder.

'The day after, we learned about the murder of Louret senior—the whole of Aix was talking about it. Gaston remembered then that his cousin had talked to him one day about certain fears his father had had about events that happened in the past, in America; at the time Pierre Louret knew very little. My lover told me: "I'm going to ask him about that first; after that, we'll talk about the inheritance; and, if he continues to make a fool of me the 'others' will take care of him." Because, Your Honour, not for a moment had Gaston suspected his cousin of any such crimes! It's all so dreadful!

'Besides, Pierre Louret was afraid of Gaston. If you ask me, that's why he carried out the crimes so quickly; he wanted to disappear afterwards and get it all over with before my lover came to settle scores.

'What's more, he killed him in the most cowardly way, without a second thought. And your colleague was his accomplice!'

'I can't allow you to use that word, mademoiselle,' I retorted. 'M. Allou allowed it to happen, that's quite different. Nothing obliged him to interfere. The definition of complicity is spelled out quite clearly in the Penal Code and—.'

'I'm not interested in your hair-splitting!' exclaimed the young woman. 'He let it happen, I consider him guilty, and I took my revenge! That's all!'

She burst out in tears once more. I waited until she calmed down before continuing my interrogation. After a moment, she continued:

'Gaston…I was waiting for him in the village. That night, because I had a premonition, I accompanied him almost all the way. Then, suddenly, they brought his body out. I managed to find the strength not to kiss him one last time—and that was hard, believe me! But I didn't want anyone to suspect me…Because, at that moment, I had decided to kill Pierre Louret, whom they had just arrested; to kill him myself, you understand, myself, outside your system of justice!

'The next morning, I learned all about the affair from the newspapers; remember, *The Marseilles Sun* had published all the details. That's how I learned of the role of M. Allou, who had anticipated the crime but had done nothing to prevent it, quite the opposite! I decided to take my revenge on him as well!'

'Do you think, mademoiselle,' I asked, 'that his role was sufficiently important to warrant his death?'

'Yes, certainly. He could have prevented Gaston's death. And, anyway, I didn't stop to think. You can't possibly understand; you don't know what Gaston meant to me. I needed to take revenge right away. Pierre Louret was in your hands and I couldn't wait; and in any case, his conviction was assured. So I decided to start with M. Allou.'

'But how did you manage to do it in such a mysterious manner? Admit it, Clement let you escape!'

'Not at all. It was all ridiculously simple, as you'll see. I got to M. Allou's building around quarter past nine, and went straight in. On the first floor there was a card on the door: Mlle. Escoiffier. On the second, I saw a nameplate: M. Allou, Examining Magistrate.

'I drew my revolver and rang the bell: nobody answered. I thought he may already have gone out and I resolved to wait for him to come back. I went up to the third floor, where I laid in wait for him to return—.'

'Why didn't you wait for him in the street, mademoiselle?' I interrupted

'Because I wanted to kill him in his own home, without witnesses and without anyone noticing me; you understand, I didn't want to be caught, because I had to kill Pierre Louret after that. Otherwise, why bother? I could simply have killed him right in the *Palais de Justice*.

'On the third floor there was one room locked, and one empty and entirely without furniture. I went into that one, where I thought I would be safe. I could see the boulevard clearly from the window. But, I had hardly got there before I heard someone ring the door-bell on the floor below. To my great surprise, because I thought the flat below was empty, someone opened the door.

'So I ran to the third floor landing and, leaning on the banister, I waited for the visitor to leave. A few minutes later, I saw three men come out. As soon as they reached the bottom of the staircase I went down and again rang M. Allou's bell; but nobody opened the door.'

'My goodness, mademoiselle!' I exclaimed. 'I know why. And my colleague's recollections were perfectly accurate. He'd been knocked out by those same individuals as he opened the door; they'd come to get the wallet!'

'Yes,' agreed the young woman, 'that's what I thought later, when I read the newspaper accounts. But, at the time, I thought he was one of the three men I had seen leaving. So, once again, I went to stand by the third floor window and wait for his return. I waited a very long time.

'All of a sudden, around eleven o'clock, I heard ringing, followed by violent knocks on the door. After waiting a few minutes I was just about to go back down to the landing to see what was going on, when a tremendous noise stopped me in my tracks: someone had just broken down M. Allou's door!

'At the same instant, the window immediately below the one where I was standing opened suddenly, and I saw a man leaning out over the street shouting for help. I realised it must be M. Allou, and I fired straight down at him from above. As I say, he had his head stuck out over the street, no doubt because of the blow he had received beforehand, from which he had probably not recovered. So I hit him in the neck and the direction of the bullet appeared horizontal, as I learnt afterwards. He collapsed. Just to let you know, I'm a crack shot and I never miss the target.

'Shortly afterwards, the crowd invaded the staircase. I had no problem mingling with the sensation-seekers and leaving the building.'

The young woman had spoken in a chillingly detached and even satisfied way.

'And you don't regret anything?' I exclaimed.

'Nothing!' she retorted. 'I was only upset when I learnt that I hadn't killed him on the spot, as I'd believed. But the Holy Virgin protected me and now he's dead. It's one of the few pleasant memories left to me after the death of Gaston!

'During the afternoon, I heard that suspicion had fallen on someone named Clement; everything seemed to point to the poor man. That was an injustice, and I have never tolerated injustice. I couldn't reveal myself yet, my task being not yet complete—having not even started in fact, because at that moment both M. Allou and Louret were still alive.

'That's when I had the idea of writing you an anonymous letter which you must have received, where I threatened you to try and make you release Clement....'

'Yes, I did receive the letter,' I said, 'but it had the opposite effect. I considered it one more charge against Clement!'

'I realise my blunder now,' admitted the young woman. 'But at the time I was almost out of my mind....'

'And why,' I asked, 'did you cut words from newspapers, since nobody knew your handwriting?'

'First of all, I didn't want to take the slightest risk until I'd finished. And also, I'd read in the newspapers that it was the method Pierre

Louret used; and I wanted to make you think that the letter had come from him, to make you more alarmed.

'On the other hand, when it came to disclosing the criminals' hideout, I didn't have the same need to conceal myself because there couldn't be any charges against me. Even so I was at pains to disguise my writing, just in case....'

'I'm curious to know how you came to suspect the refuge,' I enquired.

'Oh! That's easy. I had a bit of luck. If you remember, I told you about the man who accompanied Pierre Louret when he visited Gaston several times, who appeared to be a leader in the gang. Well, all of a sudden, the day before yesterday, I saw this man in the street; after Louret's escape, I thought I might see him around here....

'He didn't notice me. I was able to follow him at a distance as far as Pont-de-l'Arc. When I asked around, I learned that some strangers had been renting an old house called "Chateau Bastoux" for a couple of months already. It occurred to me straight away, as I'm sure it would have to you, that this hideout had been arranged by Pierre Louret with the murder of his whole family in mind. So, he was probably going to be there for quite a while: one or two years, until the affair had blown over and the surveillance had been reduced, and he could get out.'

'I agree, mademoiselle,' I observed, 'your theory sounds very plausible.'

'In that case, I might not have been able to take my revenge. That's why I alerted you. If the worst came to the worst, you would arrest him and he would be condemned to death; but, as I told you, I preferred to kill him myself.

'That's why, just before nightfall the day before yesterday, I went to hide in the woods with my motorcycle. I thought you'd be coming that same night; if Louret tried to escape, I'd be able to intervene. But the night passed without anything happening; I began to think that you hadn't taken my letter seriously.

'Eventually, towards morning, I heard footsteps. There were people walking towards the house. I moved ahead of them in the same direction, pushing my motorcycle so as to avoid running into them. At one point, they stopped and, realising that they had just surrounded the house, I stopped motionless once again, one hundred meters ahead of them.

'I had carefully reconnoitred the terrain that afternoon to determine where the woods were thickest; in case of escape, Louret would certainly take that route and so I placed myself there. I'd found a nearby path that would allow me to get away; I wanted very much not to get caught because, at that point, M. Allou was not yet dead and some were saying he might even recover.

'From the bush where I was hidden, I could see the windows of the house; I had an advantage over the police who were farther behind and couldn't see anything. I can tell you that your arrival was quickly noticed; no doubt there was a skylight in the roof, with a permanent lookout.

'You'd scarcely passed the level of the police line and could be seen on the path, when I noticed that one of the ground floor windows was opening; and I saw Pierre Louret slip outside. You, at that moment, could only see the roof of the house.

'I could see perfectly well which direction he was going to take, and I only had a hundred or so yards to crawl to be able to reach a point where I could intercept him; he had quickly disappeared from sight and I realised that he must be crawling in the bushes. Soon, I was able to follow his path by observing the movement of the leaves.

'I needed, at one point, to move another twenty meters to be exactly on his path. Then suddenly he stood up; no doubt he had seen the police and thought it would be better to run with his gun in his hand. That's when I fired.

'You know the rest. But you can't imagine my joy this morning on hearing that M. Allou was dead as well and that my mission had been accomplished!'

'That's monstrous!' I exclaimed.

But the young woman wasn't listening to me any more. She was standing up in a state of exaltation.

'Yes,' she cried, 'I've avenged Gaston. Nothing else matters. No, that's not quite true. I didn't want someone innocent to take the blame; so I came to give myself up because of Clement. And now, now....'

She was stuttering, and her demeanour was pitiful to see.

Suddenly, before I could even think of stopping her, she seized the knife I'd had shown her earlier from the table; she opened the small blade and slashed herself in the arm.

She collapsed at once and died a few moments later.

I sat there, stunned, for several minutes, overwhelmed by what had happened and what she had said...In any case, my self-respect was intact; how could I have suspected someone I didn't even know existed....

But I should, in fact, have suspected her because M. Allou had indeed discovered the truth…How had he done it? That intrigued me…

And so, admittedly neglecting my current duties, I almost ran to the hospital.

CHAPTER XV

CONCLUSION

I spent the rest of the morning at M. Allou's bedside, for he was now out of danger.

'There's still one point that's not clear,' I told him, after I had finished recounting the events of that morning. 'What happened in your flat between nine thirty and eleven o'clock: between the moment you were knocked out and the moment you were shot?'

'I have no recollection,' replied my colleague; 'or, to be more precise, I remember through a fog, as if in a dream. But we shall attempt to reconstruct what happened, with the help of the available evidence.

'At nine thirty, I fall down and someone takes the wallet. The assailants leave very quickly and I lie unconscious next to the door.

'At eleven o'clock Clement arrives and knocks very loudly. Hearing the noise, I partially regain consciousness and believe that I'm facing a new danger; or, more likely, I imagine that only a few minutes have gone by since I was attacked. I obviously feel I'm in no state to defend myself; therefore, I shoot the bolt and crawl away to call for help.

'That's when Clement hears a moan. He throws himself at the door to break it down. That rouses me further, and I stand up and, with a surge of energy, I stagger to the window to call out.

'At that very moment, Clement enters; and the young woman whom he cannot see fires on me from the floor above. I collapse before Clement's very eyes.

'And that's the whole story. It's the only possible explanation; and I do vaguely remember parts of it.'

This theory did, in fact, appear highly plausible. But how had M. Allou come to suspect who was guilty? I put the question to him.

'Oh, it's very simple!' he explained. 'I knew, and indeed I told you, that I had been struck at nine thirty; and by those fellows for whom I opened the door. You told me that someone fired on me at eleven o'clock, after having broken open that same door. And you had reliable witnesses to support your claim.

'From which I readily concluded that there had been two successive attacks.

'The first could be explained by the theft of the wallet. But the second appeared to have no ulterior motive; the crime was in fact completely inexplicable, because I was shot at the very moment that Clement turned up. He himself was obviously not responsible, because there was nothing more to be taken from my flat; and he wouldn't have chosen to kill me at the very moment the officers he had sent for were due to arrive!

'No ulterior motive?...Jealousy? I didn't suspect anyone and had received no threats.

'Revenge? Perhaps. Two people could bear a grudge against me; first of all Louret, whom I had arrested; but it seemed unlikely that, having just escaped, his first thought was about vengeance, rather than finding a hide-out. Alternatively, it could be someone connected to Gaston Richaud, whom I had allowed to be killed.

'Richaud, as you know better than I, because it was your initial investigation that established the fact, no longer had any family; therefore, it would have to be a mistress. Furthermore, the information you received from Lyon revealed that he was living with a certain Louise Blanchi. She certainly would have a cause for revenge against me, but doubly so against Pierre Louret who had actually killed her lover. That's why I told you I could see the beginnings of an explanation, which would be given credence if we were to learn that Pierre Louret had been murdered.

'And that's exactly what happens; and someone catches a glimpse of a sixteen-year old youth fleeing the scene—which can equally well be a twenty-year old woman.

'Then you inform me that the same weapon has been used in both crimes. Who would want to kill both Pierre Louret and me? Who would want to avenge themselves on both of us? There was only one common factor: the death of Gaston Richaud. There was no longer the shadow of a doubt: the identity of the culprit became glaringly obvious.'

'But,' I asked, 'how did you guess that she would give herself up on learning the news of your death?'

'Oh, that didn't surprise me at all. She had, by her anonymous letter, tried rather clumsily to save Clement; so she did show some sense of fairness. And also, someone who has taken two other people's lives for revenge doesn't place a high value on their own. I was sure she wouldn't leave an innocent person to die; it was enough to let her think that her mission was over.

'In any case, it didn't cost us much to try, before embarking on a long and complicated search which wouldn't necessarily have accomplished anything. And during which Clement would have still been in prison....'

M. Allou fell quiet and I took it to mean that he was tiring. I rose to leave, but he signalled to me to stay.

'I feel fine,' he said. 'I was thinking of that young woman...I didn't think she would kill herself...And, in a few months from now, her sinister designs on me would have started to wane and would have eventually disappeared...How she loved him! Don't you find that wonderful? No, you're young, you don't yet know the value of love....'

'But still,' I exclaimed, 'you were only saved by a miracle!'

'Yes...But, you see, the first error was mine. I shouldn't have let Gaston Richaud be killed. I wanted some proof against Louret, and my hunter's instincts took over. I repeat what I told you the other day: a magistrate's job is to think. I had discovered the truth sitting in my office, just as I found it this time from my hospital bed....

'If I'd stayed there, I wouldn't have got carried away and allowed Richaud to be killed...I was wrong, and I paid for it...I feel sorry for that poor child....'

'I'm convinced,' I said, 'that if you pushed her to confess, it was not to protect yourself but to save Clement, who stood accused by circumstantial evidence.'

'That's true enough. In this last business, I was no longer a magistrate, but a victim – that's to say a private citizen. I had the right to keep my theories to myself. And I wouldn't have said anything, had not an innocent man been accused.'

'But then,' I replied, 'she could have attacked you again, and this time she would no doubt have succeeded.'

M. Allou didn't reply, and I left the room.

There's not much more to tell about this frightening affair.

Needless to say, I interrogated the five individuals arrested at "Chateau Bastoux," but to no avail. No doubt they had prepared their stories in advance, because they had not been allowed to communicate with each other, yet there were no discrepancies between their statements.

They claimed to have been paid—and handsomely—by an unknown man to rent the villa and shelter the criminal. They denied any involvement in the theft of the wallet or Louret's escape.

These denials struck me as plausible. Obviously, the escape had been organised by them; but it was no doubt executed by men who didn't stay in the area afterwards. Besides, none of the witnesses to the scene in the *Palais de Justice* recognised any of the accused.

As for the attack against M. Allou, nothing proved they were involved in any way.

I was obviously aware, because of the statements that Gaston Richaud's mistress had made, that one of the gang leaders was among them. But which one? It was no longer possible to tell, because the young woman had taken her secret with her. I strongly suspected the one who had spoken to me at the beginning, and who seemed like the leader; but a simple opinion is not a basis for judicial proceedings.

This same man, incidentally, made a curious revelation which I feel obliged to record to shed more light on the affair. When he explained to me that his role was to shelter the criminal for a considerable sum of money, I could not help commenting:

'But that's despicable! No sum of money in the world could justify sheltering such a monster...After all, he slaughtered his whole family just for money; in other words, simply to become a playboy...'

My respondent shrugged his shoulders.

'Did you know so little about him?' he replied. 'He confided in me during the several days of forced intimacy we endured together. He hoped that with the money he could become the number one gang leader in the whole of Europe. Would a simple playboy have such a goal? Louret had an insatiable ambition and a monstrous vanity! That's what it was all about!'

In the end the only charge we could bring against the five men was that of harbouring a criminal. On this count they received the maximum sentence: two years in prison.

As for the wallet, it was never found.

Who had hidden it? Obviously, persons who knew of its existence and whose names could be found in it.

Newspapers all over the world had reported what had happened at Cypress Villa. The day after the death of Louret senior—in other words, the day before the attack on M. Allou—the special editions had commented at length on the first disappearance of the famous wallet. Then the next morning *The Marseilles Sun* had, among its other revelations, stated that the papers had remained in the hands of my colleague. It is likely that those who made them disappear had nothing to do with Pierre Louret's gang; it was the settling of old scores.

As for Clement, it goes without saying that he was released immediately. But he refused to talk about the twenty-thousand francs found on his person; he even denied the existence of the famous night-time enquirer.

I mentioned it to M. Allou, who laughed.

'Surely you've guessed?' he said. 'It was obviously Clement who gave *The Marseilles Sun* all the details of our discussions and all the explanations you heard in my flat. The mysterious night-time enquirer was none other than a journalist, and the twenty-thousand francs was the price of the information. That was the reason that Clement was so insistent on going to Cypress Villa and staying there as long as possible. But he's never going to admit that!'

'It was only a minor offence,' I remarked, 'because what you told us was not supposed to be a secret. Why didn't he admit it as soon as he was accused of murder? His silence could have cost him his life!'

'He was counting on my testimony to prove his innocence,' concluded M. Allou. 'He believed that I knew more about the attack than I actually did. He would only have spoken after my death, as a last resort...The poor devil...It was just bad luck that I was shot just as he broke open the door...That's what you get for being too greedy! For I'm sure that he came to my place after Pierre Louret's escape so as to get a story for the newspapers. What can you do? When one is born jinxed....'

'You're too kind to him. It was you that worked it all out, and you that was in danger; and he's the one that reaps all the benefit!'

M. Allou placed his hand on my shoulder and said solemnly:

'But that, dear boy, is the story of our chosen profession.'

THE END

APPENDIX 1

THE FRENCH LEGAL/POLICE SYSTEM

In the British and American systems, the police and prosecution gather information likely to convict the suspect. The defence gathers information likely to acquit the defendant. Arguments between the two, and the examination of witnesses, are conducted in open court, and refereed by a judge. The winner is decided, in most important cases, by a jury of ordinary citizens.

In the French system, also adopted in many other continental countries, all criminal cases are investigated by an examining magistrate. He or she is a jurist independent of the government and the prosecution service, and is given total authority over a case: from investigating crime scenes; to questioning witnesses; to ordering the arrest of suspects; to preparing the prosecution's case, if any. Much of the "trial" of the evidence goes on in secret during the investigation (confrontations between witnesses; recreations of the crime) working with the police. The final report of the investigating magistrate is supposed to contain all the evidence favourable to both defence and prosecution.

Investigations are frequently long—two years is normal in straightforward cases—but trials are mostly short. Witnesses are called and the evidence is rehearsed in court, but lengthy cross-examination in the British/American style is rare. In the *Cours d'Assises*, which hear serious criminal cases, there are nine jurors, who sit with three professional judges: other criminal cases and appeals are heard by panels of judges alone.

In France, as in Britain, the defendant is theoretically innocent until proven guilty. But in practice there is a strong presumption of guilt if an examining magistrate, having weighed the evidence from both sides over a period of several years, sends a party to court.

There is no right of *habeas corpus* in France. Examining magistrates have a right (within limits) to imprison suspects for lengthy periods without trial.

Much of the leg-work during an investigation is done by the police (in towns) or *gendarmerie* (in rural areas), but relations between magistrates and police are not always as good as depicted here. Not only did anyone below the equivalent of Chief Inspector have to defer to the examining magistrate but in the 1930's they also had to cope with the Brigade Mobile – the equivalent of Scotland Yard's Flying Squad, but on a national scale – which could swoop down and usurp their powers without warning. Not surprisingly, their morale was terrible.

There are other differences between police and *gendarmes*. The police (called *Police Nationale* since 1966; before that it was known as the *Sûreté*) are under the control of the Ministry of the Interior and are considered to be a civilian force. The *Gendarmerie Nationale* is under the control of the Ministry of Defence since Napoleonic days and is considered to be a military force. In addition to policing smaller towns and rural areas, it guards military installations, airports and shipping ports.

Under French law, you cannot disinherit certain heirs *(les parts réservés),* which you can under Anglo-Saxon law.

APPENDIX 2

VINDRY ON THE DETECTIVE NOVEL

1. 'Le Roman Policier.' Article in Marianne, 26 July 1933

There is much talk at the moment about the detective novel; a little too much. Some praise it to the skies: and when they let go it will crash. Others relegate it to the basement: it will become covered with mould and quickly rot.

Can't we allocate it its just place? Not too high, so as not to make promises it is unable to keep, and avoid disappointment. Not too low, so as to avoid a sense of unremitting decline and the abandonment of all quality.

But in order to be fair about it, we have to recognise what it is. So many judgments have been made about it that, in reality, have nothing to do with it.

The "Detective Novel"! Under this perhaps badly-chosen heading have been lumped totally disparate works; works not without merit, certainly, but not destined for the same public and therefore sowing fateful confusion.

As with the Christmas cracker, everyone was hoping for something else and curses their luck.

Under this heading, adventure novels have been published and called detective novels on the pretext they feature criminals.

The adventure novel is about chance, the unpredictable, fantasy science and the last-minute revelation which upsets all calculations.

The detective novel is rigour, logic, real science and a solution relentlessly deduced from the given facts.

Two genres more different it is impossible to imagine.

The adventure novel is a treasure in a labyrinth; one finds it by chance after a thousand surprising detours. The detective novel is a treasure in a strong-box; one opens the door very simply with a tiny, necessary and sufficient key.

The former must present the complexity of a panorama; the other that of an architectural drawing.

The detective novel must be constructed like a mathematical problem; at a certain point, which is emphasised, all the clues have been provided fairly; and the rigorous solution will become evident to the astute reader.

No, the presence of a criminal is not enough to turn an adventure novel into a detective novel.

Conan Doyle and Gaston Leroux, in several works, were the masters of the detective novel; Wallace, that of the adventure novel.

Something else as well, delivered under the same heading: the police novel.

It includes shoot-outs, rooftop chases, opium dens, made-up detectives and cries of horror.

The detective novel, on the contrary, economises on revolvers and the police chases of pre-war films.

It lets you into the dining-room, with the meal already prepared, and not into the kitchens.

It is not a work of realism or a documentary; it is constructed for the mind. The logic is unreal, or rather, surreal. The master of fact and not its slave.

One cannot accuse it of an "unhealthy influence on youth," for it interests only the intelligence.

So we have three essentially distinct genres:

The adventure novel, about the life of the criminal.

The police novel, about the arrest of the criminal.

The detective novel, about the discovery of the criminal.

And even, dare I say, "discovery" pure and simple: for the criminal and the police are mere accessory elements to the detective novel. Its essence is a mysterious fact which has to be explained naturally; the criminal hides his activities and the detective tries to discover them; their conflicts provide convenient situations: the "givens" of the problem. That's it.

True detective novels are only "police novels" by accident. Maybe we should change the name.

I propose: "Puzzle novel." (1)

Does this confusion between the detective novel, the adventure novel and the police novel result solely from a badly-chosen term?

No: they all three possess a common element of fascinating importance: action. Overwhelmed by the speed, one no longer notices the body moving.

(1) *Roman problème*: "problem novel," or "puzzle novel" (less confusing).

Action dazzles the reader. Alas, it sometimes dazzles the author: of what use is style if the intrigue is enough to excite passion? Superfluous dressing which can only slow down the chase.

Style, however, is not a gilded ornament to be taken out of the wardrobe on festive occasions; it must be true to itself to the end. An umbrella has its own style if it remains perfectly umbrella.

The detective novel has a right to its own style, just like everything else. It can demand its own language, for it stutters in the others.

Its phrasing must be unadorned, the better to fly with the action.

Its narrative must contain everything necessary, but nothing more.

The detective novel, as opposed to the psychological one, does not see the interior but only the exterior. "States of mind" are prohibited, because the culprit must remain hidden.

It's only necessary to reveal what can be seen *immediately* in the action; but to do it properly, by which I mean rigorously; look for the aspect which has impressed the spectator to the crime.

"The cry of horror" is a bit vague. And generally inaccurate: gendarmes very seldom let out cries of horror; and the civil police scarcely more.

No, a detective novel isn't necessarily "badly-written."

It can, incidentally, possess other qualities; one only needs to read the marvellous "atmospheres" of Simenon, who has imposed his intensely personal touch on the genre.

But I've only tried here to bring out the salient aspects of the detective novel or, if you will allow me, the "puzzle novel":

An action;

An equation;

A style.

Perhaps it will then be easier to assign it its proper place.

No, it's not very high: it doesn't lift the spirit in any way; it's a sort of crossword: a simple game of intelligence.

No, it's not very low; it seeks to tap into our need for logic and our faculties of deduction. There's nothing shameful about that.

It's an honest and respectable genre: nothing grandiose and nothing unhealthy. One can, without shame, experience pleasure or boredom equally well. But it's ridiculous to venerate it or despise it.

It can be the source of works that are bad, mediocre or good: and even brilliant if they are signed by Edgar Poe—but they contain a "special something," it's true; even so it's important to acknowledge that Edgar Poe used this mould in which to pour his "precious metal."

2. Extract from a 1941 Radio Française broadcast

"Why did I give up the detective novel? For no particular reason: the way one gives up a game one no longer finds amusing. Because the detective novel is nothing more than a game; nothing more and nothing less. Like chess and crossword-puzzles, it has its rules, which constitute its honesty and dignity. I tried my best to play by them and was only interested in the logic: in the problem properly posed and correctly answered."

"In the puzzle?"

"Yes, in the puzzle. Much more so than in the drama or the adventure. I wanted to excite the reader's intellect more than his passion. I don't regret in any way having written detective novels. It was a game where I didn't cheat. If I stopped writing them it's because the game had ceased to amuse me, and one shouldn't write when one doesn't feel like it."

"Can you identify the reason for this change of heart? Or does it remain obscure, even to you?"

"I think I understand. It's gruelling work, but with moments of sheer pleasure and more fascinating than any other game. But now that I'm writing real novels—."

"*Les Canjuers*, *La Cordée,* and last year *La Haute Neige?"*

"Yes, since then I no longer play with my characters, I collaborate with them and I live with them. It's a solemn joy, far from amusement."

3. Extract from Letter to Maurice Renault, editor of "Mystère-Magazine" October 26, 1952

What's the oldest French detective novel? I believe it's Voltaire's "Zadig." A short novel, but rather too long to be a short story.

It conforms to what I believe to be the definition of the genre: "A mystery drama dominated by logic."

So, three elements:
1. A drama, the part with the action
2. A mystery, the poetic part
3. The logic, the intelligent part

They are terribly difficult to keep in equilibrium. If drama dominates we fall into melodrama or worse, as everyone knows; if mystery dominates, we finish up with a fairy tale, something altogether different which doesn't obey the same laws of credibility; if logic dominates the work degenerates into a game, a chess problem or a crossword and it's no longer a novel.

A great example of equilibrium? "The Mystery of the Yellow Room."

Made in the USA
Monee, IL
13 April 2020

25820946R00085